A LONG AWAITED KISS

"I finished all of the mudding in all of the suites today. Mudding's a bother, so I think I deserve to celebrate, too."

She could feel a smile form. "Do you? What do you have in mind? A back massage?"

"That would work . . . if you're naked . . . and in bed."

She stretched. "I am tired."

"I don't intend to let you sleep."

She looked him up and down. "You *do* look sexy in your torn jeans." She rinsed their tea mugs and put them in the dishwasher. Then she started for the stairs, swinging her hips more than usual. "I'd never want to be called a fair-weather friend."

He grinned. "I didn't think so. You're more like a friend in need."

The thought of Brody in her bed sent her nerves buzzing. "Fair is fair. You're always there for me."

She pushed her door open, and when he stepped into the room, she smashed him against the wall for a fierce kiss. The fun and games were over. She'd thought about this for too long . . .

Books by Judi Lynn

Cooking Up Trouble

Opposites Distract

Published by Kensington Publishing Corporation

Opposites Distract

A Mill Pond Romance

Judi Lynn

LYRICAL SHINE
Kensington Publishing Corp.
www.kensingtonbooks.com

LYRICAL SHINE BOOKS are published by

Kensington Publishing Corp.
119 West 40th Street
New York, NY 10018

All Kensington titles, imprints, and distributed lines are available at special quantity discounts for bulk purchases for sales promotion, premiums, fund-raising, educational, or institutional use.

Special book excerpts or customized printings can also be created to fit specific needs. For details, write or phone the office of the Kensington Sales Manager: Kensington Publishing Corp., 119 West 40th Street, New York, NY 10018. Attn. Sales Department. Phone: 1-800-221-2647.

Lyrical Shine and Lyrical Shine logo Reg. US Pat. & TM Off

First Electronic Edition: July 2016
eISBN-13: 978-1-60183-785-1
eISBN-10: 1-60183-785-2

First Print Edition: July 2016
ISBN-13: 978-1-60183-786-8
ISBN-10: 1-60183-786-0

Printed in the United States of America

ACKNOWLEDGMENTS

I'd like to thank my agent, Lauren Abramo, for keeping me on track and for sharing her expertise and acumen with me.

I'd also like to thank my editor, John Scognamiglio, for being so pleasant to work with and Rebecca Cremonese, for making copy edits so pain-free.

And as always, I owe thanks to my wonderful beta readers: my daughter, Holly, and my critique partners Mary Lou Rigdon and Ann Staadt. Thank you!

Chapter 1

Harmony Meyer listened to the pleasing male voice on her GPS. She was getting close to Lakeview Stables, Ian and Tessa's resort. Fields blanketed with snow spread out on both sides of the highway, the banks close to two feet high, but the road was plowed and decent to travel. The weather had been mild all through December, but once January shook its wintry head, the snow had started. At least she didn't have to fight ice, or she'd have stayed home rather than risk life and limb.

At a stop sign in the middle of nowhere, she noticed two horses in a fenced-in pasture. One of them looked satiny and honey-colored. The other had brown spots on white, just like her neighbor's rat terrier back home in New York. Mist billowed from the horses' nostrils, and Harmony smiled when they turned to race to a nearby barn. A man crossed a driveway toward the big, red building. Their owner? Her thoughts wandered until the sharp sound of a horn jerked her gaze behind her. A forbidding, dark SUV with tinted windows lurked close to her bumper. Damn, when did he get there?

With a casual wave to the driver behind her, Harmony returned her attention to the road and followed the route her nice GPS man told her. She frowned when the black SUV took every turn she did. Should she be concerned? What if the driver was a serial killer who followed innocent, young women on Indiana back roads to scare them half to death? She snickered. She was far from innocent. Besides, she'd taken a self-defense class and carried pepper spray. Too bad for him.

When she turned into the wide lane that led to the main lodge, the big, black beast of an SUV did the same. The hairs prickled on the back of her neck. What were the odds two people would arrive at a nearly deserted resort at the same time on the same day? It was the middle of January, the resort's dead time. Her friend, Tessa Lawrence, had guaranteed she'd mostly have the place to herself. She parked near the front door and hurried toward its entrance. Before she could reach it, Tessa stepped outside to greet her.

"Harmony!" Tessa's tangle of copper hair glowed in the sunlight. Her lips curved in a smile. A tall, gorgeous man with black hair and a lean build stood beside her. Must be the new hubby.

Harmony looked him over and gave a low laugh. Scrumptious. She shook her head at her friend. "No wonder you ditched your single days."

Tessa made the introductions. "Harmony, my husband, Ian. Ian, my writer buddy, Harmony. We always go to the same writers' conferences and room together. Then we stay over a few days for sightseeing."

Ian grinned. Major heartthrob. "So, you're the one who writes about witches and werewolves. Tess says you write romances like hers, but scarier."

"And a hell of a lot sexier." Harmony gave Tessa a considering look. "But that might change now that she's married."

A car door slammed and Ian turned his gaze to the dark SUV. A hulk of a man—maybe a body builder—carting two heavy suitcases with ease, walked toward them. Ian grinned. "Brody!"

Tessa opened her arms to greet him. "Harmony, this is Ian's big brother. He owns a construction company, but since business is slow this time of year, he came to help Ian divide the west wing of the inn into four more rooms."

Brody's hair was as dark as his brother's, but his eyes were a cool, smoky-gray instead of warm brown, and his build bulged with muscle. Intimidating.

She straightened her shoulders. No one would intimidate her ever again. Brody studied her quickly and dismissed her. Must not like blondes with blue eyes . . . and attitude.

Harmony raised her chin. To each his own. Probably just as well, though. She didn't come here to flirt. If she didn't write like a mad woman, she'd miss her deadline. Unthinkable. She'd work twenty-four hours a day if she had to.

Damn the landlord of her building. He'd taken it into his head to get rid of the old boiler and redo the entire heating system. In January. Go figure. Lots of dust and noise. Not conducive to concentrating and letting her subconscious untangle plot lines. She tried going to a coffee house to work on her laptop, but she was too nosey, got distracted by watching people come and go. So Tessa had suggested she come here. For free. Tessa wrote during the winter months, too. They'd eat together every night and yak like they did at conferences. How could Harmony refuse?

Brody shrugged broad shoulders. "You guys can make small talk out here in the cold if you want to, but I'd rather go inside where it's warm." He stalked away.

Ian turned to her. "Sorry. I should have offered to get your bags while you and Tess wait in the lobby. I'll be there soon." He stretched out his hand for her keys and strode toward her Jeep. His boots crunched on the salted drive.

Harmony stopped to admire the lodge—a flagstone house with white trim and a red tin roof. It stood three stories high in the center with a wing off each end and red double doors in its center. "No wonder Ian loved this place the minute he saw it."

A golf course stretched to the east of the parking lot, and stables and paddocks to the west. The lake lay in back with log cabins dotted along the east shore.

Tessa glowed with pride. "Sam, the previous owner, kept the exterior in great shape, but nothing had been done inside for over a decade. It needed lots of work. We're pretty proud of how it turned out." She led Harmony into the warm, comfortable lobby with gleaming maple floors and high, beamed ceilings.

Harmony glanced upward with a grin. "No bats?" Tessa had told her the story of Ian and his nocturnal visitor.

Tessa laughed and shook her head. "Only the one, and that was enough." She pointed to hooks along the inside wall. "If you want to leave your coat here, you can. Then it's handy."

Brody had dropped his suitcases on the floor near the front desk, tossed his wool coat on a hook, and sat on one of the plush, brown leather sofas in front of the fireplace. He stretched his long legs before him. His gaze fastened on Tessa and he smiled. "How's life with my brother?"

She went to perch on a forest-green chair across from him and motioned for Harmony to take the seat next to hers. "I still kinda like the guy."

Brody laughed. "That's good. The family signed you up for life. We don't take returns."

When Ian draped his jacket over the back of the couch and sat next to his brother, Harmony had a chance to study them more thoroughly. Both men would turn heads. Tall and dark-haired, they exuded maleness.

Ian motioned toward her suitcases. "When you're ready, I'll show you to your room. I put you on the top floor, far enough from our project that we shouldn't disturb you."

Brody turned his attention on her again. "I noticed your license plate. You're from New York?"

She nodded. "The Finger Lakes region. That's why I drive a Jeep. Winters can get serious there."

"I live near Ithaca, too."

She frowned. How odd that they'd both traveled to the same spot in Indiana from the same area in New York. Fate? Nah. No stars were stupid enough to throw her and Brody together. He already made her nervous, he was so intense.

The dark brow rose again. "If Ian had told me you were coming here, I could have offered you a ride." He sounded as appalled by the idea as she felt. She grinned. He could have, but it wouldn't have happened.

She gave her head a quick shake and crossed her fingers. "I'm staying a month until my apartment building's finished. You probably won't be here that long."

He stared. "Actually, I am. Ian's project is going to take a while. This is the only time I can help him. I go to our parents' place for Christmas and the holidays, and then business picks up in March."

She didn't hide her lack of enthusiasm that well. Why should she? He wasn't exactly doing somersaults about enduring her company. "We probably won't see that much of each other. I'll be at my laptop all day."

Tessa beamed at the two of them. "Actually, you two will be coming to our house for supper most nights. That way, we'll get to spend some time with you."

Harmony's shoulders sagged; Brody's stiffened.

Oh, goodie! She stifled her sarcasm. If only she were as nice as Tessa. She'd make an effort. She'd be the epitome of charm. They'd eat together, then Ian would drag Brody off to talk about guy things, and she and Tessa would cozy up somewhere to yak. Harmony was fully capable of civilized behavior when the need arose.

The front door opened and a woman with two children interrupted their conversation. Harmony stared, surprised. The woman had dyed black hair pulled up in a clip, a nose ring, and more tattoos than Harmony could count. She looked out of place in this rustic setting.

"Hi, I'm Paula, Ian's cook."

Before Harmony could respond, the little girl—maybe five, with black hair like her mother's—ran straight to her and wrapped her in a hug. "You look just like Princess Elsa in *Frozen*."

"*Frozen*?" Harmony blinked.

Paula laughed. "You must not hit kids' Disney movies. Bailey's in love with all things about Arendelle and the two princesses."

Bailey plopped on Harmony's lap and said, "This is so cool! You look like Elsa and Tessa looks like Merida from *Brave*."

Harmony made a mental note to look up both of the movies on her laptop. Merida must have wild, red hair if she looked like Tessa.

"Move it, kid!" Paula motioned for her daughter to scoot toward their apartment in the inn's east wing. Harmony had heard a lot about Paula and her kids from Tessa—all good. When Paula's son, maybe ten, got close to Harmony, he stopped to look her up and down, too.

"Do you like kids?" he asked.

Oh, lord, what was she getting herself into at this resort? She gave him a level stare. "Why? You aren't going to put a toad in my coffee cup, are you?"

His eyes went wide, surprised by her answer. "Mom would ground me."

Harmony smiled. "Then we'll get along great."

"Mom says you write books. You must like them."

Okay, she hadn't seen that coming. "I have a few favorites."

"Would you read to us?"

"My books?" Her voice rose. Her vampires tended to be a bit horny, not good reading material for kids.

"*Harry Potter*."

She pursed her lips, considering. She'd never cracked one of those books. Probably missed out on a cultural milestone. "What time? I have to hit my page quotas every day before I do anything." But after she wrote for five or six hours, her brain went to hell. She was lucky if she could think of two-syllable words. A break would be good for her.

"Before supper?" He narrowed his eyes, waiting for her answer.

She'd be shot by then, brain dead. "Hell, why not?"

The boy smiled. "I'm Aiden. The book has long chapters."

"Tough luck. I can give you thirty to forty minutes. I have a short attention span." Especially when it came to kids. Harmony looked at Paula. "Is that all right with you?"

Paula's grin widened. Mimicking her, she said, "Hell, why not?"

Ian laughed. "I have a feeling you guys are going to get along fine."

"Just come up and knock on my door when you're ready," Harmony said. "That will help keep me on a schedule. When I start writing, I lose track of time."

Paula herded her kids to their apartment, and Harmony let out a sigh. She turned to see Brody studying her once again. She grimaced. "I know. I probably shouldn't cuss in front of kids."

"You made that kid a promise. You're going to keep it, right?" His voice sounded flinty, judgmental.

Harmony struggled with her temper, but didn't tamp it down completely. She gave him a look, her voice equally sharp. "I don't make promises I don't keep . . . to anyone. Why do you think I came here? I'm trying to keep my promise to my editor and get my damned book to him on time."

He raised his eyebrows. "You should have red hair like Tessa. It sounds like you have a temper."

"It's different. Blondes only hiss when we're provoked."

"If you say so. The blondes I've met are frivolous."

"Then you meet the wrong ones," she snapped.

A smile tugged at his lips. "I'll have to remedy that."

Oh, crap. What had she done?

Chapter 2

Ian carried Harmony's bags to the third floor and opened the door to her room. "Tessa insisted you have this one because she said it was your favorite color."

Harmony raised a hand to her lips. The room took her breath away. "It's beautiful." The walls were painted a soft apricot and the gleaming wood floors were dotted with braided rugs. A mini-fridge nestled under a small counter with a coffee pot. White curtains framed a wide window that looked out over the lake at the back of the property. Right now, a layer of ice covered it. In the distance, she could see small specks of people ice fishing. A desk sat before the window, and two overstuffed chairs in the corner invited settling in with a book. A fluffy, white bedspread was made even cozier with a peach-colored throw angled over the footboard.

Ian grinned. "I'm glad you like it. Tessa thought you'd want to get settled. Brody will drive you to our house for dinner at six."

"He's staying in the inn? Tessa said he was staying at your house."

"We invited him to. He didn't think that was right when Tessa invited you and you were staying here."

"Does he always do what he thinks is right? He never bends the rules, even to spend more time with you guys?"

Ian laughed. "Brody's the oldest kid of our brood. I have two older sisters, Bridget and Maeve. I was the baby. Brody felt it was his duty to keep us in line."

"The authoritarian. I get it."

"We made his life hell." Ian turned to leave. "Tessa said to tell you that she made gumbo. Said that was guaranteed to get you there on time."

Harmony licked her lips. "One of my favorites. Tessa and I were on panels together at a romance conference in New Orleans. I came away craving Creole, Cajun, and all things spicy."

When Ian left, she reached for the case that held her laptop. She could put her clothes away later, but while she had an hour or two and her mind was fresh, she could slip in a little writing time. She kicked off her shoes and wiggled her stockinged feet. Time to get comfortable and settle in.

She'd written the book's hook and the first six chapters, but hadn't taken the time to edit them. She'd introduced Serifina, the witch protagonist, and her future romantic interest, Luxar—a vampire. They'd each been fighting an unknown enemy in their city. The reader knew that they both battled Torrid, a powerful vampire with ruthless ambition, and soon, they'd collide to work together to save Portside.

She was wading through rewrites when a knock on her door interrupted her. She glanced at the clock. *Holy shit.* Five thirty. She pushed the save button on her computer and went to see who was there. Aiden wouldn't show up for story time the first day she got here, would he?

Brody glowered down at her. "Looks like Tessa was right and you got lost in your writing world. She phoned and asked me to check on you."

He made it sound like an accusation. She shrugged. "It's what I do. I don't usually stop until my stomach growls. I'm not used to a schedule."

"But you do try to be considerate of friends and hostesses?"

This guy could be a real dick. She crossed her arms. "I had my phone alarm set for five forty."

She barely got the words out when the alarm went off. "Oh, baby, baby, my baby, baby" sang through the room.

Brody raised his eyebrows. "Whatever gets your attention."

She ground her teeth, then frowned at him. "You cleaned up." He still wore his worn, comfortable jeans, but he'd changed into a button-down shirt and sweater. He'd be yummy if he weren't such a sourpuss.

He looked her up and down. "I guess I didn't need to bother." She hadn't changed out of her driving clothes—faded jeans with a few rips in the right thigh area and a baggy sweater. Her hair was still pulled back in a low ponytail.

"I didn't know gumbo meant a formal dinner." She yanked at the scrunchie that held her hair, letting loose waves cascade past her shoulders.

Brody stared, then shook his head. "No matter. Shall we? It's time to go." In the lobby, he waited for her to shrug into her winter coat and then walked with her to his SUV. She wasn't short, but the step-up to get into the passenger seat was more exertion than she was used to. He gave a grim smile, enjoying her effort. He'd be surprised to know how much she walked back home. She was in good shape, whether he thought so or not, damn the man!

When she fastened her seat belt, he shut the door and circled the vehicle to slide behind the steering wheel. On the drive to Tessa's, she mentally calculated how much time they'd have to spend together. Not all that much. Her stay here looked better.

Harmony grinned from ear to ear when they pulled into the driveway. The wide bungalow was as charming as she'd pictured it. White, with green shutters and flower boxes, it looked warm and welcoming. She reached for the door handle, but Brody shook his head. What now? He walked around the SUV to open her door for her. She stared at him. "Are you for real?"

"I am, but I think you've lived with vampires and werewolves too long to remember some of the social norms."

"No one opens doors for women anymore."

Brody shrugged. "They should."

A thick layer of snow blanketed the yard and the house's roof. It looked like something on a Christmas card—inviting and cozy, especially since the sidewalks were cleared. Harmony hurried up the path.

Tessa threw open the front door before they reached it and pulled Harmony inside. "I can't believe you came. I'm stuck on a scene in chapter eleven. Where are you in your book?"

Ian rolled his eyes and waited for his brother to join them. "Tessa promised not to talk writing while we eat."

Brody smiled. "I'm sure she keeps her promises, just like Harmony claims she does."

"I heard that!" On her way to the kitchen, Harmony threw him a dirty glance.

Ian grinned. "You got in trouble."

"Yeah, I'm worried now." Brody hung his pea coat on the coat tree by the front door, carefully wiped his feet on the welcome mat, then trailed behind them. He sniffed as he went. "Mmm, something smells good."

Harmony twirled in a happy circle in the kitchen. "I can't believe you remembered. We ate this together in New Orleans when we skipped out for a few hours between panels."

Tessa pointed to the oven. "Do you remember what we had for dessert?"

"You didn't!"

Tessa opened the oven door a crack. "Bread pudding with whiskey sauce."

Harmony hugged herself.

Brody shook his head. "For being thin, both of these women *really* love food."

"And you don't?" Ian opened the refrigerator to grab a bottle of wine and two bottles of beer.

Brody accepted one. "That's Mom's fault. She cooked a meal every night, and every meal came with dessert."

"Then this will feel just like home." Ian motioned for him to help carry heavy pots to the round, cherry wood table. Trivets waited for them. Tessa sat across from Ian, Brody across from Harmony. Oh, good, Brody could watch her eat. When they were all seated, they dug in.

Tessa's bungalow lived up to everything Harmony expected. White cupboards lined three walls. Granite countertops provided plenty of workspace, and the oak floors looked worn and homey.

Ian pointed his spoon at Brody. "Fill me in on what everyone's up to at home."

Brody told him about their parents and sisters. "Maeve's youngest boy—"

Ian interrupted. "How old is Connor?"

"Four now, he broke his arm after Christmas. Got a sled from Santa and went down the wrong hill."

Tessa winced. "Is he all right?" She glanced at Harmony. Harmony had broken her arm as a kid when her brother pushed her off their backyard swing set.

"Kids heal fast, but he hates his cast. Itches. It's a good thing Maeve can work on her bookkeeping from home."

"And Bridget?" Ian glanced at Tessa's copper hair. "My sister's the woman who gave redheads a bad name. What a temper!"

"She's fine. Likes her students this year. No one's blown up the chemistry lab yet." Brody paused for a second. Voice low, he said, "Cecily remarried on New Year's Day."

Ian fumbled his fork. "The bitch talked another man into marrying her?"

Harmony felt her eyes go wide. She wasn't good at hiding her feelings. Tessa turned to her and whispered, "Brody's ex. Ugly divorce."

Harmony had wondered. He looked to be about forty and didn't wear a ring. Either he'd always been a woman-hater or he'd recently become one.

Tessa reached over to touch Brody's hand. "I'm sorry. That had to be hard for you."

He grunted. "Not really. They'll probably make it to happy-ever-after. She married someone a lot older with loads of money. I've heard he loves to dote on her."

"Everything on her bucket list," Ian said.

Harmony asked, "Is she a blonde?" The man certainly had a low opinion of them. Maybe Cecily was the reason.

Ian answered. "No, a ball-buster brunette." He obviously didn't like Brody's ex.

Harmony raised her hands in defeat. "I guess females in general don't cut it. Blondes are bubbleheads, brunettes bust balls, and redheads have fiery tempers. Brody likes Tessa, though. So maybe a girl has to have copper hair to pass inspection."

Brody quirked an eyebrow. "Why? Are you interested in giving it a go?"

"Me? No, just asking out of curiosity."

Brody focused on her. "Have you been married? In a serious relationship?"

Those smoky-gray eyes made her squirm. "Not my thing. I get distracted too easily."

"No heartbreak in your past?" he persisted.

Tessa glanced her way. She looked uncomfortable. "She wouldn't allow that."

"None at all?" Brody sounded surprised.

Harmony shrugged. "A drummer once stole a carton of cigarettes from me when he left before breakfast, but that was good. I meant to give up smoking anyway."

His lips curled in a half-smile. "So you've stayed single out of convenience, and I'm single because I got screwed over."

Convenience? Hardly. More like self-preservation. When you let someone touch your heart, they had the power to control you. "Looks that way." Harmony scooped up a forkful of rice, but he wasn't finished.

"Do you want to find someone someday?"

She shook her head. It was safer to keep people at a distance. Except Tessa. Writing had drawn them together. "I'm happy doing what I do. Why complicate it?" He'd made her curious, though. She couldn't help it. She'd always been nosey, even before she started writing. "You?" she asked.

He nodded. "I want someone who's smart, funny, loves to cook, loves to entertain, and wants to have children."

"That's why you bugged me about my promise to Aiden." The words popped out before she could stop them. When would she learn to be more discreet, to let conversations die that were getting uncomfortable?

"I wanted to have kids. Cecily didn't. She *said* she did, but she kept putting it off."

Smart Cecily. "Kids aren't for me. They're even more bother than a man."

Ian laughed. "Do you have a pet? Anything?"

"I feed pigeons on my window ledge every morning after breakfast."

Brody stared. "And that's enough for you?"

What did he want from her? She could make up a story. She was good at that. She could tell him that she baked cookies to take to the homeless every weekend and that she rescued strays off the street. But she didn't need to impress him, so she might as well be honest. "When I'm lonely, I meet up with friends or go to a bar and sit on a stool next to someone. It works for me."

"One night stands?"

Ian shook his head. "Brody . . ."

But Harmony didn't mind. Her life wasn't all that exciting. He'd yawn before long. "No, I only need lust when I finish writing a book. Sort of a celebration."

He shook his head, frustrated. "I've never met a woman like you."

"Consider that a blessing." But fair was fair. She told hers. He should tell his. She asked again, "You?"

He grimaced. He was more private than she was, she could tell. "Occasionally."

She gave a knowing nod. "Once in a while, we just need a human touch." She took the last bite of her meal and glanced toward the bread pudding.

Tessa grinned. "You've always had a sweet tooth."

Brody stood to collect dirty dishes and carry them to the sink. Did the freaking man do *everything* right? Ian cleared away the leftovers and brought the bread pudding to the table. Their mom must have trained her boys well. They knew their stuff.

Ian steered the conversation to small talk while they finished up. Then Tessa shooed the men from the kitchen, and she and Harmony rinsed and cleaned so that they could sit at the table, bump heads, and yak writing.

Serious, ready for shoptalk, Harmony asked, "So what's the hang-up in chapter eleven?"

"The scene I planned just won't work." Tessa did a quick rundown of her new book, her characters, and where she was stuck.

They brainstormed until Brody wandered out from a back room around ten. "We'd better get back for the night. Ian and I are starting work early tomorrow morning. We have a lot to get done in a month."

Harmony stretched and yawned. "I have a lot to do, too." She bent to hug Tessa. "See you tomorrow. Can I help with anything? Come early to set the table?"

"Nope, I'm enjoying myself. Just show up on time for supper." She raised an eyebrow at Brody. "You'll have to pry her fingers off her keyboard."

"Got it." He held out Harmony's coat for her, then shrugged into his own. When they stepped outside, the wind hit them, blasting off the lake. It picked up snow and pelted them.

"Damn, it's cold!" Harmony hustled for the SUV. She hopped inside and slammed the door before she remembered Brody's rules.

The man didn't get to do door duty this time, but he looked mighty relieved when he slid behind the steering wheel. The warmth of the SUV thawed her on the short drive back. He pulled close to the doors of the resort and started to get out, but she was too quick. She dashed out of the car and into the lobby before he could stop her.

She could get used to having a man deliver her almost to the front door, but she'd better not get too comfortable with it. It wouldn't happen at home. She waited inside the lobby for him. He looked surprised to see her when he stepped into the foyer. "I thought you'd zip up to your room."

She grimaced. "I might not be traditional, but I have some manners. Thanks for the ride."

He frowned at her. "Ian told me your favorite color is apricot."

She blinked. Where the hell had that come from? How did this man keep throwing her off balance? "Yeah, I guess it is."

"That's so feminine. You're . . ." He hesitated.

She gave his arm a playful punch. "No worries. I get it. I'm not."

They said their goodnights and went their separate ways. Once in her room, Harmony went to the window to watch white flurries swirl outside. A storm was blowing toward them, intense enough that she couldn't see to the other side of the lake. She closed the blinds and changed into her pajamas. Then she crawled into bed, dragging her laptop with her. She balanced it on the bedspread and finished the rewrites of the chapters she'd been working on, but her thoughts kept drifting to Brody. Had he been hopeful, madly in love when he married his Cecily? And what had she done to him? A reason, Harmony reminded herself, she avoided happily-ever-after. Because it was a crapshoot whether or not it would work.

Chapter 3

When Harmony turned on her computer the next morning, there was an e-mail from Tessa. *Coffee cake outside your door.* She looked at the time and grinned. Ian must have brought it over when he came to work with Brody. She'd stayed up later than she meant to last night, but it was worth it. She'd gotten her rewrites done and added to them.

She cracked the door and looked up and down the hall. No one in sight. A good thing. Her hair would make Medusa's—on a bad day—look good. She wore men's pajamas that she could swim in, and her ratty pink robe brought her all sorts of comfort, but wouldn't win any prizes. It matched her ratty, pink slippers.

She grabbed the goodie and retreated back into the room. She'd brought her favorite coffee with her from home, so she started a pot. She was set. Carbs and coffee were her kind of breakfast. She sent back a quick e-mail. *Thanks! You're the best.* She knew, for sure, that Tessa was sitting in front of her computer, still in her PJs and a robe, with coffee and carbs, too. That's why they were such good friends.

When the pot quit gurgling, she poured herself a cup, cut a slice of coffee cake, and settled in front of the keyboard. Her fingers itched to get started. She'd finished the first fourth of the book last night. *Only* one fourth. That left about forty-five thousand words to go, about one hundred ninety-five pages. Ugh. She bit her bottom lip. If she wrote ten new pages a day . . . Oh, hell, she'd have to, or she wouldn't have time to do a final rewrite. Who was she kidding? She should really write fifteen pages a day. The book was due on February twentieth.

Fretting wasn't going to put words on the page. She took a gulp of coffee and looked at her plot notes. Serifina, her protagonist witch, was walking into trouble. She just didn't know it. A new player had come to town, a rogue vampire who kept nasty company. Harmony was writing like a crazy woman when someone knocked on the door.

Buggers! Why now? Luxar, her hero/vampire, (and soon to be love interest) was about to rescue Serifina from the bad guy, whom he'd been keeping an eye on. Things were getting tense. Torrid was ready to leap.

Another knock. She glanced at herself in the mirror. She could scare small children. She sighed, but she'd seen Tessa in the morning. Her hair went crazy, too. Ian should be used to it. She got up and opened the door. It wasn't Ian. Brody stood there, staring down at her. *Oh, shit.*

He blinked at her. Okay, he'd been married once. Surely, Cecily had days when she looked like a harridan. Then again, maybe not. The woman sounded like Miss Sterility—always perfectly coifed and made up. She probably woke up with fresh breath. Harmony ran her tongue over her teeth. Gross, she hadn't brushed them yet. Brody took a quick breath, then said, "Just wanted to let you know we had to turn off electricity for a short while to rewire a wall. It won't be long. We didn't think about warning you, but we should have."

She felt her shoulders sag. The man *did* do everything right. Always did the responsible thing. How hard would that be to live with? No wonder he picked Cecily. She shook her head. "No biggie. I'm not doing any research. I have plenty of battery left. I can still write."

Brody looked repentant. She liked that expression on him. "I don't have your cell phone number, so I couldn't call you to let you know."

"No problem. Really. Don't worry about it." Luxar was calling to her. Her vampire couldn't wait to spring into action. A battle was brewing. She flashed Brody a fake smile. *Go away, nice man!*

He frowned. "Are you all right?"

"Great, why?" How bad did she look? Okay, she didn't want to know. It couldn't be good.

Brody studied her. "You seem all pent-up, like something's bothering you."

She stared. The man read people better than she'd thought. "I'm getting ready to write a fight scene. Two vampires are going to rip and tear at each other. I can't wait."

Brody took a step back. He thought she was crazy, she knew it. "And that gets you all worked up?"

Harmony tried to explain. "If I'm not all hot and bothered, how can I expect my readers to be?"

He thought about that. "So you live vicariously through your characters."

She sighed. "When I'm writing about them." She wasn't some nerd who didn't have a life. Okay, she might be a nerd, but she had friends and went places.

He gave a quick nod. "Okay, then, I'll let you get back to it." He turned to leave, then stopped. "Almost forgot. Ian said to tell you that the lodge is closed for two weeks until we get the big stuff done in the west wing, but Paula will still fix lunch for us. We won't see Tessa until dinner. That way she can write. You two must share some of the same habits."

Harmony nodded. "Writers write."

"Lunch is at twelve thirty," he said. He glanced at her oversized pajamas and frayed robe. With a small shake of his head, he retreated.

Harmony tried to run a hand through her hair. Tried. It was too tangled. Brody didn't understand that when a scene called to you, you *had* to write it. But why should he? He probably thought she was batty *and* nuts now. Damn.

She was trying to make nice with Tessa's brother-in-law, but she had a suspicion this wasn't going to be a victory. She went back to her writing.

Serifina *thought* she was rushing to help a member of her coven, but it was really a trap. When Torrid leapt from a rooftop and pinned her to a wall, he caught her by surprise. Before she could react, though, Luxar—with his vampire speed—stood behind Torrid and yanked him off her. Then all hell broke loose. Fangs ripped. Claws slashed. Serifina had no idea who was who, or whom to help.

The words flew as fast as the action.

When Torrid finally popped away—damn old vampires who could transport—she was annoyed with herself. When Harmony reread those words, Luxar was beginning to look a lot like Brody—tall, muscled, brooding, and intense. But then again, what vampire wasn't? The kicker was when he looked at Serifina and his eyebrow rose with disapproval. Harmony sighed. Oh, hell . . .

Chapter 4

An hour later, her cell phone rang. She glanced at it. Brody. "Just wanted you to know the power's back on."

"Thanks." She glanced at her WiFi signal. Yup, there it was. She didn't want to talk. The words were flowing. She repeated, "Thanks for letting me know."

He hesitated. "You'll remember that lunch is at twelve thirty, right?"

"A given, I'll be hungry by then."

He didn't sound convinced. "Okay, see you then." He took his pledge to Tessa of keeping her on track very seriously. What *didn't* he take seriously?

Harmony cut another slice of coffee cake and poured herself the last cup of coffee. Where had she left off? Oh, yeah, after Luxar's nemesis fled, Luxar dragged Serifina to his mansion so that he could protect her. If Torrid wanted her, there must be a reason. Serifina went with him, but didn't intend to stay. She didn't need a babysitter, but she did need answers. She informed him that she was a witch, a powerful one, who could take care of herself.

Luxar remained unconvinced. "Like you were protecting yourself from Torrid?" His smirk looked a lot like Brody's. Harmony blocked that thought. Serifina, however, was intrigued.

"I was chanting a protection spell," Serifina told him. "I didn't need your help."

The two started arguing, and Harmony decided to use the scene to feed some background information into the story. Luxar was explaining Torrid's bloody history to Serifina—a history that shocked Harmony with its violence—when someone knocked at the damn door again, interrupting her thoughts.

She came here for quiet! But she struggled to stay civil. "Who is it?" she called.

The door opened and Brody stepped inside. He ran a hand through his black hair when he saw her, clearly frustrated. He pointed at the wall clock. Twelve forty. "Lunch?" he reminded her.

Damn it all to hell! How did that happen?

His tone was patient. "I know you don't like formal, but do you usually eat lunch in your pajamas and bathrobe?"

"Yes, actually." She blew out a breath in frustration. "Look, just eat lunch without me. I'll drive into town and grab something later."

"And ruin supper at Tessa's?" Was the man *always* this logical? He glanced at his watch. "Tessa told me to keep you on track."

She narrowed her eyes at him. "Is that why you're staying in the lodge instead of staying at their place?"

Brody avoided the question. He motioned toward the bathroom. "Throw some clothes on and come on down. We'll save you a sandwich."

She stared at him. "I've lived on my own for a long time now. I can take care of myself. You don't need to babysit me. Go over and stay with your brother and Tessa, and I'll meet you all for suppers each night."

Brody crossed his arms and planted his feet. He had the look of someone who meant business. It reminded Harmony of the many times she'd been called down to the principal's office. Unyielding authority. Voice soothing, as though talking to a two-year-old, he said, "I'm already settled in. Now move it. I'm not leaving without you."

She stared. Was he serious? He sure as hell looked like he was. She couldn't move him without a bulldozer. She could throw a fit, but it wasn't really her style. And besides, he was Tessa's brother-in-law, and Tessa loved him. So Harmony sighed, punched the save button on her computer, and stalked into the bathroom. She came out in the same ragged jeans and oversized sweater she'd worn yesterday. He'd hate that, she knew. But he only gave her a quick glance, then hustled her into the hall. They walked down to the dining room together. At least she'd given her face a quick scrub and brushed her teeth.

When he held out a chair for her at the table, she pressed her lips into a tight line. He made her feel small. Not just size-wise. The top of her head stopped at his shoulder. But he had a way of making her feel like a naughty child again. She hated that. When she sat down, he scooted the chair in for her. *Good grief!*

Ian and Paula watched with amused expressions. Then Ian looked at her hair yanked back in a rubber band and her face with no makeup, and he burst out laughing.

"That's the last straw!" Harmony was ready to throw her stuff in her bag and drive home.

Ian shook his head. "You look like Tessie when she's hit a sweet spot in her manuscript and the scenes are coming to her."

Brody stared. "Tessa loses track of time, too?"

"You have a lot to learn, brother." Ian reached for his napkin. "Once Tessa settles into writing mode, the world could blow away outside her windows, and she'd never notice from nine to five. I think she used to write nonstop until she married me. Now she quits when I come home, and we cook together."

Brody slanted a sideways look at Harmony. "So that's normal."

Ian grinned. "As normal as writers get, as far as I know. But I've only lived with one, and she's pretty much worth it."

Brody frowned, and Harmony could almost see him adding up the pluses and minuses.

Ian said, "If I'm late getting home, Tessa doesn't hassle me. Hell, sometimes she doesn't even realize I'm late."

"That was one of Cecily's pet peeves." Brody reached for his sandwich. "She always made plans for the night—meeting someone for dinner or attending some function. Even when she knew I worked long hours in the summer, she had some place she wanted to go, someone we should meet for drinks or dinner."

Ian winced. "Sounds like Lily."

Brody gave him a knowing look. "That's why I warned you off her."

Both brothers went quiet a moment, thinking.

Harmony looked at Paula. She needed a change of subject. "This sandwich is delicious. A Cuban?" There was roasted pork and ham with melted cheese. "Bet it's fun just cooking for the kids at supper while the inn's closed for two weeks."

"The kids love it. We have the whole evening to ourselves." Paula touched her hand to a locket. She opened it so that Harmony could see baby pictures of Aiden on one side and Bailey on the other. "I'm so lucky. Our lives have been bumpy, but they've been cool with it."

Harmony looked around the dining room. "This is a beautiful room." An oak floor gave it a country feel, but crown molding added more sophistication. Windows lined the back wall, looking out over the rolling lawn and the lake. Cream-colored walls brightened the space. Impressionistic landscapes added soothing color.

Ian beamed. "Tessie helped me decorate the whole place. She made it into what I'd pictured."

Harmony nodded. "She's good at that. Visited my place once when she came to New York to see her agent. When she left, she'd done all these little things that made the apartment look better."

"You don't have the touch?" Brody asked.

She shook her head. "No talent at all. I can look at colors and fabrics, but I can't picture how any of them would go together."

"That's me," Ian said. "Brody's good at it, though."

"I have to be," Brody said. "If I build a house for someone and they know how they want it to feel, I need to make sure things come together."

Harmony disagreed. "I think you either have the gift or you don't. You must have it." And once again, she was lacking in something Brody excelled at. Surprise, surprise! It was like the Universe made him just to annoy her.

She expected to see a superior smirk on his face, but Brody's attention was drawn to something outside the back windows. His brows furrowed in a worried frown. He narrowed his eyes, staring at the lake. "Is that one of your ducks?" he asked Ian.

Ian finished the last bite of his sandwich and followed Brody's gaze. His expression took on a worried look, too. "Is she stuck in the ice?"

Brody stood to go see her better. "She's struggling, but can't get out."

A feather could have knocked Harmony over when Brody disappeared to get his winter coat. Ian followed him. She looked at Paula. "Are they going to rescue a duck?"

"Not just any duck," Paula told her. "Ian fed it all summer and fall."

Brody glared as he passed Harmony. "You can't just leave a poor animal trapped in ice to die, whether you fed it or not."

The two men tramped out the back door and headed to the lake. Harmony turned to Paula. "How do you unstick a duck?"

Paula pursed her lips, thinking. "It can't be that thick there. That's where the channel empties into the lake. The water's usually moving. Could you pour hot water on the ice to make it melt?"

"Let's find out." Harmony started to the kitchen and Paula hurried after her. They filled two huge soup pots with hot water and put them on the stove to boil.

Harmony glanced out the window to watch the men. "How long do you think the duck's been there? I wonder how she got stuck."

"It got really cold last night. I bet she was in open water when the sun set and by the time the sun came up this morning, the water had frozen." She went to get her coat. So did Harmony. They each grabbed a pot and carried them out to the men. By the time they reached them, Brody had a hand auger and was drilling holes around the duck. Ian had an old-fashioned saw and was trying to saw the ice between each hole. He'd made deep enough grooves that when they poured the boiling water on them, they melted a decent amount of ice without harming their feathered friend.

"Can you bring more?" Brody asked.

"We started two more pots," Harmony said. The women trudged back to the lodge and started a chain of boiling water to bring for the men.

The duck, Harmony was surprised to see, seemed to realize that they were trying to rescue her. They finally cut a circle in the ice and could pick it up and carry it, with the duck trapped in it, into the barn. Horses whinnied when they entered, and one stretched its neck for a treat. Ian went to a bucket with a lid and handed each of them a carrot. They dutifully pampered each horse and rubbed its nose before they returned to the stranded duck. Brody had turned on a heater and placed her close to it. Her ice started melting and soon was thin enough, he slammed his fist on it, and it broke. The duck wobbled, unsteady on its webbed feet. Brody immediately reached for her, held her close so that she wouldn't be frightened, and carried her outside. Then he looked at Ian. "What should I do with her?"

Ian looked up and down the shoreline. Some ducks swam farther down the channel. The water was open there. The men walked her down to them and let her loose. She hurried to her friends.

When they returned, their boots muddy, their coats filthy, they both looked frozen. Harmony shook her head. "It looks like they need hot chocolate."

Paula led her into the kitchen and they got busy. Soon, they sat around the dining room table again. This time, they each cradled a mug of hot chocolate to warm their hands.

Brody raised an eyebrow at her. "We had a dog when we were little. It was our job to take care of it."

"How your mom instilled so much responsibility in you, I have no idea." Harmony's parents preached a lot of virtues, gave lots of lectures, but most of them didn't take. Of course, her parents weren't that responsible themselves, so maybe that made a difference.

Ian looked outside the windows to where they'd rescued the duck. "Lady fell into the weedy side of our pond once and got tangled up. We had a hell of a time pulling her out of there."

Brody and he locked gazes. "We almost lost her," Brody said. And the memory still bothered him, Harmony could tell. Maybe she'd judged him wrong. Maybe he wasn't the Authoritarian. Maybe he was Mr. Responsible. For Everyone. No one could describe her that way. She was Miss Disappear.

Brody frowned at her. "I'm thinking you don't get that attached to your pigeons."

She could feel a blush climb to her cheeks. She shrugged.

He leaned forward, surprised. "You do, don't you?"

She'd never told anyone. Her friends would have a good laugh at her expense. "You know how pigeons are. They bob around the sidewalks, begging for scraps all day. One got scared and flew in front of a car. When the car kept going, I could see him on the street, dragging his left wing and walking funny. I went down and caught him and took him to a vet."

Paula was staring at her. "A pigeon?"

"He was *my* pigeon," Harmony clarified.

"And?" Brody prodded.

She grimaced. "The vet said his wing wouldn't get better, his leg was gone. He'd never walk or fly, probably wouldn't last the week. So I paid to have him put to sleep."

Paula gaped, but Brody gave an approving nod. "Cecily never understood about pets, but nothing should suffer if there's a way to avoid it."

Oh, boy, Harmony hadn't thought about that pigeon for a long time. The vet had given her the same look Paula had. In the city, pigeon lovers were scarce, but she'd fed that damned bird every day for over a year. He trusted her. She shook her head. Not that many people would understand. She finally looked at the clock. "Oh, lord, I've lost a lot of writing time. Gotta go. I want to get more pages done before the kids come up." How many had she written this morning? Six. She had nine more to go.

"I could tell them to forget it tonight," Paula said. "You can put it off another day."

She was tempted, but shook her head. "No, I promised them. Send them up. I have a few hours, and I know what the next scene is. It's all there. I'll get enough done." Maybe. Hopefully. Harmony gave a quick wave and started up the stairs. She went straight to her computer, and the words flowed.

Luxar told Serifina, in no uncertain terms, that she wasn't leaving his house. Serifina started for the door, and Luxar—with his vampire speed—was standing before it, blocking her way. He laughed and said, "Let me show you to your room." She raised her palms and blasted him out of her way. Luxar rubbed his chest. Not so funny now. He raised a dark eyebrow—just like Brody liked to do. Hmm, Harmony paused, her fingers over the keys. Did she have Serifina blast Luxar because it made her feel good? If she had magic, would she zap the smug look off Brody's face? She shook her head. Nope, the zap worked for the story.

Luxar finally explained that he was only trying to help Serifina. She had no idea how powerful Torrid was and how evil. Their enemy had lots of friends in low places. She could use an ally. Serifina listened to him and realized it would be a major battle to leave Luxar's mansion. She'd pretend to agree with him, and then she'd sneak off later. Luxar showed her to her room—extravagant, of course—and . . .

Harmony paused, reading her dashed-off plot points to see what should happen next. She was mulling over ideas when knocks sounded on her door. She glanced at the clock. Five p.m. Kid time!

Chapter 5

Harmony saved her work and stood to greet the kids. She'd gotten six more pages done. Only three short. They ran to her, excited.

"Ready?" Aiden handed her the book—*Harry Potter and the Chamber of Secrets*.

Harmony frowned. "This is book two. I've never read the first one. I won't know what's going on."

"Mom thought of that." He handed her a DVD. *Harry Potter and the Sorcerer's Stone*. "She bought us the movie to watch. She said we could watch half today and finish it tomorrow before we start reading the book."

"Your mom's brilliant. She thinks of everything." With Aiden's light brown hair, light brown eyes, and a spattering of freckles across his nose, he reminded her of one of the kids on the cover. That boy had red hair, but the same sweet, sort of innocent look. Bailey was almost an exact replica of her mom—a little Goth princess.

Harmony popped the movie into the machine, closed the window blinds, and got comfortable in one of the easy chairs in the corner. Aiden hopped on the unmade bed and sprawled on his stomach. Bailey climbed onto Harmony's lap.

It was a good thing that Harmony kept the remote close by, because Aiden kept interrupting the movie. "Did you see that?" he demanded. "How Dumbledore took the lights from the lamps and put them back?"

"Pretty cool," Harmony admitted.

A little later, he pushed himself onto his knees and cried, "See all of those owls, trying to deliver letters? Guess what happens!"

"A dragon flies over and eats them all?"

Aiden stared. "Dragons don't eat owls."

Harmony shrugged. "I must have forgotten that."

Aiden jumped to his feet when Hagrid knocked down the door to bring Harry a birthday cake. He couldn't sit still. A few scenes later, he called, "Hey, stop the movie there! Did you hear what kind of wand Harry got? One with a phoenix feather. Do you know what a phoenix is?"

"Of course, I do! I'm a fan of Greek myths." Harmony gave him a dirty look. "Give me a little credit."

He was too busy with his next thought. "Later, when you meet Hermione, her wand's core is dragon's heartstring, just like Viktor Krum's. You'll meet him later, too, and Draco Malfoy's has a unicorn hair."

"Wonderful, but if you don't stop talking, we're never going to finish the movie, not even the first half of it."

"Okay, I'll shut up. I want you to get to the part with Harry's familiar."

Harmony pushed the play button and Hagrid gave Harry the beautiful, white owl. "Wouldn't it be neat to have a familiar?" Aiden interrupted again. "If you could have anything, anything at all, for a familiar, what would it be?"

She paused the movie again. "A werewolf."

"You can't have a werewolf!" Aiden told her. "Werewolves are too big."

"You said I could have anything."

"Anything that's smaller," he amended.

Bailey bounced on Harmony's knee. "I want a canary!"

Aiden let out a loud sigh. "How could a canary help you if you're in trouble?"

"It can sing me to sleep at naptime."

"Not that kind of trouble! If something attacks you."

Harmony shook her head. "I'm keeping my werewolf."

"You can't keep a werewolf." Aiden sat up on the bed, prepared to argue, when he looked up and saw Brody. Brody was standing in the doorway, watching them, with an odd expression on his face.

Oh, lord, what did she miss this time? Harmony glanced at her watch. "Oops, It's five forty. I have to be at Tessa's soon. You two need to scoot."

"But we didn't make it halfway through the movie!" Aiden complained.

"And whose fault is that?" Harmony asked. "*Someone* won't stop talking."

"But we can't start reading the book until we finish the movie," he explained.

Harmony sighed. "Okay, just this once, get your asses to my room at four, but you have to zip it, or we still won't get done." She'd be shaving off an hour of afternoon writing time, but she'd make it up at night.

Aiden solemnly zipped his lips, then grinned. He turned to Brody. "Do you want to watch it with us? It's a good movie."

"I'm helping Ian . . ." That's as far as he got. Bailey ran to throw her arms around his leg.

"Please. Daddy used to watch movies with us."

Brody's expression crumpled. "I guess I could take one afternoon off."

Bailey squealed her delight.

Aiden grabbed her hand and tugged. "I just remembered. Mom told us to be back at five thirty. We're going to get a lecture."

They took off and Brody shook his head. "We just got steamrolled by two little kids."

Harmony laughed at him. "They're experts. They stay awake nights plotting on ways to train adults."

It was his turn to look at the clock. "We'd better get moving. We're supposed to be there at six."

Harmony glanced down at her jeans and sweater. She touched a hand to her hair, pulled back in the rubber band.

"You have no idea how cute you look," Brody said.

Harmony stared.

"You're one of those women, like Tessa, who doesn't need makeup. Cecily always looked too perfect. Always. Now, come on. We're going to be late."

His compliment settled somewhere in her chest and spread warmth through her entire body. She meant to thank him, but he'd already turned and started down the hallway. It was a throwaway. Just a comment. She ran to catch up with him. They both bundled into heavy coats, scarves, and gloves at the front door before they stepped outside. The cold was so crisp, it hurt to breathe. He'd already driven his SUV close to the front door and had it running to warm it up.

She did her usual dash to the passenger door and slammed it shut, so that he could hurry to slide behind the steering wheel.

He glowered at her. "Usually, I'd insist on holding your door, but for right now, thank you. It's freezing out there."

"No biggie."

"Cecily would have taken her time getting in and out of the car until my teeth would chatter. It was a matter of privilege."

She wrinkled her nose. "It's none of my business, but your Cecily sounds like a real pain in the ass."

He threw back his head and laughed. "As a matter of fact, she was."

When they got to Ian and Tessa's, Ian greeted them at the door. He hurried them inside. "Tessa's dragging a little today. She's in the kitchen."

Harmony went to check on her. "You all right?"

Tessa shrugged. "I've been pushing the writing pretty hard. I might have to slow down a little."

"How far are you?" Harmony braced herself. She knew she'd be jealous.

"Over half way. You?"

"Don't ask."

Tessa pressed a hand to her stomach. "I forgot to eat lunch."

Harmony nodded understanding. A common occurrence for her. "Need any help with anything?"

"No, Ian helped me set the table. Everything's ready to go."

The meal—meatloaf and mashed potatoes—was delicious, as usual.

"It's one of my favorites," Brody said. "Thanks, Tessa."

"You're one of *my* favorites," she told him. "Thanks for coming to help with the remodeling."

The men shooed them out of the kitchen after they ate. "Brody and I always did clean up at home," Ian said. "Go somewhere and talk writing."

Tessa stopped to give him a quick peck on the cheek, and then she and Harmony settled in the sunroom at the back of the house. Ian had installed a heater to take off the chill. Tessa's flowerbeds and herb gardens were buried now, but the yard was still pretty with its white picket fence and bird feeders. The fence poked above half a foot of snow.

Harmony did her best to perk up her friend, but Tessa looked done-in. Neither of them would win any beauty pageants tonight. Tessa's copper hair was scraped back from her face with a hair band. She hadn't bothered with makeup either. Harmony asked, "How's the book coming? Are you unstuck? Middles are my nemesis."

Tessa wrinkled her nose. "My hero's being a real jerk right now. He's supposed to be. He's stupid-jealous, and I'm ready to smack him."

Harmony laughed. "How soon before you like him again?"

"Two more chapters, if he lives that long."

"It's never a good idea to kill off the love interest half way through a book." Harmony tilted her head, studying her friend. "Maybe you're trying to do too much. You're baking on weekends for your bakery, but you make desserts for Ian's lodge, too. There's only so much time and energy to go around."

Tessa blew out a frustrated breath. "That's the thing. The resort's closed right now. I don't have to worry about afternoon teas. I should have *more* energy, not less."

Harmony didn't have any answers. Finally, she said, "Let's call it quits early tonight. You cooked for me. You don't have to entertain me. Get some rest."

Tessa fidgeted, unhappy. "You came all this way to see me, and I'm fizzling on you."

"We're friends. Through thick and thin, good and bad . . ."

Tessa laughed. "Thanks, but I've looked *so* forward to seeing you. I'm bummed."

"You'll see me tomorrow, and every night for a month. We can manage." She went in search of Brody, and they drove home early.

He parked the car, and she waited for him in the lobby, like she always did. When he clomped into the foyer and left his boots on a floor mat under the coat hooks, he seemed restless, at loose ends. Finally, he asked, "This is going to sound a little strange, but there's a large screen TV in the library. I don't suppose you'd let me watch the beginning of your Harry Potter movie, would you? Then I'll know what's happening when we watch it with the kids tomorrow."

"Only if you let me watch it with you." She shouldn't. She *should* go to her room and pound out three pages. But it was only three pages. She'd get them done. She'd never missed a deadline, and she wasn't going to start now. "Aiden talked so much, I couldn't keep track of things."

His eyes lit up. "I'll make popcorn while you get the movie."

She headed up the stairs, and he headed to the kitchen. They settled on the sofa in the study and watched up to where Hagrid gave Harry the snowy owl as a familiar.

Brody shook his head. "Kids' movies aren't like I remember them."

"What do you mean?"

"That poor kid gets treated like crap, and his enemy wants to kill him."

Harmony took the last bit of popcorn and emptied her wine glass. "Every Disney movie kills off the mom or parents in the first five minutes. Sometimes sooner. How else can the kid be the hero? And a stepmother's never nice to them. Kids like to think they can overcome anything."

He stretched his legs and leaned back to get more comfortable. His thigh muscles bulged beneath his worn jeans, and his long-sleeved tee clung to his torso. A very nice torso, Harmony decided. She should have put ice in her wine to cool herself down. He tilted his head, considering. "I guess I never thought about parents getting in the way."

She was about to answer when his cell phone rang. He glanced at the caller I.D. and grimaced. "I have to take this. My sister Bridget."

Harmony nodded and stood. She stacked their popcorn bowls and glasses and headed to the kitchen. When she returned, he was still on the phone, his expression serious. She gave him a quick wave, grabbed the movie, and went upstairs. Time to pay the Piper. She opened her laptop and got busy.

Chapter 6

Harmony stretched to wake up. She opened her eyes to soft apricot walls and white, country curtains. How spoiled could a girl get? She lay there a few minutes longer as thoughts swirled in her head. A whole scene sprang to life, and she tossed off the blankets to get to her keyboard. While the laptop loaded, she yanked on her old robe and slid her feet into her slippers. Time to crank the heat a little higher. She turned it down at night, preferring to sleep in a cool room.

She opened the blinds on the window to find a swirl of patterned ice painted on the glass. Jack Frost must have been busy last night. The weatherman had predicted below zero temperatures. She hoped Ian's duck was huddled someplace safe.

The coffee pot spit a final shot of steam to let her know it was finished, and she went to pour herself a cup and slice another piece of Tessa's cake before hitting the keys. Luxar and Serifina were clamoring for attention.

Serifina waited for nightfall, then snuck from her bed. She cracked the door to her room, determined to escape. Luxar was leaning against the wall, waiting for her. They bantered. Sexual tension crackled. It *was* a paranormal romance, after all. Luxar slammed her against the wall, and she let him. Their kiss was passionate. They decided to work together to defeat Torrid and his friends.

Harmony glanced at the clock. She'd been writing for almost two hours. First rewrites, then fresh pages. Her muscles felt cramped. She slipped into the hallway, pacing up and down it to get rid of some of her nervous energy. Rip saws buzzed through wood in the west wing. She could picture Brody cutting and handing off boards to Ian. Hammers pounded. A nail gun made quick work of something. She wondered how much progress they'd made.

Progress. Something that wasn't happening in the hallway. She sighed and returned to her laptop. Serifina and Luxar were feeling a little frisky.

The bed was only a few steps away from the door. After all, they *were* a team now. Harmony could smell sexual tension. Luxar lifted Serifina up and carried her into her room, but stopped suddenly. Stared at her. "Torrid's on the move. He's stalking someone." Serifina didn't have to ask him how he knew. Vampires had telepathy, could scan mortal minds. And he'd focused on Torrid enough to know when his emotions ran high. They left the mansion together to find him.

Harmony's stomach growled. Her last scene was a tease. It stretched Serifina and Luxar's lust to new levels. Her stomach grumbled again. She went for another slice of coffee cake. An hour later, she drained the coffee pot. Her fingers couldn't keep up with her ideas. Then "Oh, baby, baby . . ." startled her out of her fantasy world. Her cell phone!

"Yes?"

Brody's deep voice announced, "It's eleven thirty. If you want a shower today, this might be the time."

"Eleven thirty? Really?" How did that happen? But when she looked at her page numbers, she'd finished five more pages. That took a while.

"See you at lunch."

Before he could hang up, she said, "Thank you. I mean it, but I hope Ian's paying you extra to keep tabs on me." She genuinely appreciated his call. Without a reminder, she'd be in the same grubby jeans and baggy sweater she'd worn since she got here.

His voice dry, Brody said, "Ian pays me in brotherly love."

She had to laugh. "Does that go for your carpentry work, too?"

"It covers everything. See you soon." And he disconnected.

When she walked into the dining room at twelve thirty, Brody looked at her, surprised. She smirked. Her hair waved past her shoulders, shiny and clean. She wore black jeans and a black, fitted, long-sleeved tee with the words *I put a spell on you* across her breasts. She'd put on mascara, blush, lipstick—the works.

"Well, who knew?" Brody smiled up at her.

She grinned. "You didn't think I'd get my shit together, did you?"

Paula had made chicken salad sandwiches for lunch today, and Brody dug into them.

Ian shook his head. "Those are one of his favorites."

The man had good taste. She followed suit. Half a sandwich down, she wiped sauce off her mouth. "They're really good." She turned to Ian. "How's Tessa? Better today?"

"Still moving slow. We made a simple meal for tonight. I helped her slap rub on baby back ribs and put them in the oven on low. I'll add sauce when I get home and throw in some potatoes, then crank up the heat."

Brody looked concerned. "She doesn't have to cook for us every night. We can manage on our own."

"No, she wants to," Ian said. "She's looked forward to seeing you guys since you agreed to come. She's going to cut back a little on her writing so she can enjoy you."

"But she only writes in the winter. She runs the farm stand in the summer." Harmony nodded to Brody for support. "If you don't mind eating a little later, Brody and I could drive over at six and help with the cooking."

Brody stared at her, surprised. "Do you cook? I mean, something people can eat?"

Offended, Harmony raised her chin. "I'm not an expert like Tessa, but when I have friends over, I have a dozen tested recipes I can count on. They've never complained. No one's gone to the hospital."

Brody winced, and she studied him. Had she hit a nerve? Good, he deserved it. "I can't cook," he said, "but I'd be happy to help out."

Ian waved away their offers. "I can help Tessa, too, but she'll fuss about it. For right now, she's just tired, so I can fill in."

Paula chimed in. "I could make dinners for Brody to take over."

Ian sighed. "Thanks, guys. Really. But it's your two-week vacation, Paula. You're not cooking. If worse comes to worst, we'll drive into town and eat at the diner."

"That works for me." Harmony finished her sandwich. "I came here to visit with Tessa, not to make her entertain me."

Brody nodded, but Ian shook his head. "Tessa's not ready for any of that yet. You'll lose this battle."

"She *is* a redhead," Brody said. "We'll try again later."

On the way back to her room, Harmony fretted. She didn't want to wear Tessa out. She knew her friend. She'd try to be the perfect hostess, and she didn't have to. But try telling her that.

Chapter 7

Brody, Aiden, and Bailey knocked on her door at four o'clock. Brody tried to corral the kids so that they didn't rush her, but with no luck. After hugs and rushed greetings, they settled in for the movie—Aiden on his stomach on her bed—she'd made it since Brody was coming—and Bailey on Brody's lap.

Harmony glanced at gauze wrapped and taped around Brody's thumb. "Cut yourself?"

Brody scowled. "Ian hired Luther for afternoon help. The kid's a fast learner, but his first swing with a hammer didn't hit its mark."

Ouch! That had to hurt.

Bailey touched her finger to her lips and then touched Brody's wound. Harmony went gooey inside. What a sweet kid! Brody's expression melted. The man was Bailey's to do with as she pleased.

Aiden was in a hurry to start. Actually, he was in a hurry to finish. They had to watch the movie before Harmony could start reading the book to them. "You have the movie ready to go where we left off, right?"

Harmony gave Aiden a stern look. "If you talk through every scene, we won't get finished today."

Eyes gleaming with mischief, he zipped his lips. Damn, he was a cool kid! Every once in a while, he'd get so excited about a scene, he'd turn to blurt something to her, but Harmony would pretend to zip her lips, and he'd grin and zip his, too. Near the end of the movie, when Harry and his friends made it past the three-headed dog, Brody's eyebrows shot up when Professor Quirrell removed his turban, and Voldemort's face was implanted on the back of his head. He turned to ask, "Snape's working with Voldemort, too, right?" But Aiden raised his finger to his lips and hissed, "Shhh!"

Brody scowled, but obeyed.

When the movie ended, Aiden jumped to his feet on the bed, shot his arm into the sky, and yelled, "Yes! Tomorrow we can start the book."

"You don't stand on beds," Brody growled.

Aiden immediately plopped onto his fanny.

"Tomorrow, yes." Harmony pointed to the clock. "But for now, get moving. You're late again."

Aiden groaned. "Mom can't get mad at us for ten minutes."

"Don't push it. Get out of here," Harmony told him.

Bailey grabbed Brody's hand and tugged on it. "Will you walk with us when we go downstairs?"

"Yeah, and tell Mom the movie just ended," Aiden pleaded.

"Sure." Brody did more than that. He lifted Bailey onto his shoulders, and the little girl giggled. He had to duck to clear the doorway, then turned his head to tell Harmony, "I'll start the SUV. We're cutting it close again."

She rolled her eyes. At home, everything revolved around her writing. That's the way she liked it, but she hustled to get ready. She'd gotten five pages finished before the kids came up and was feeling pretty happy with herself.

They pulled into Tessa's driveway at six, sharp. Harmony was grateful they'd had such a short drive. There'd been a dusting of snow today, and the road was slick. When she got out of the car, the sidewalk was slippery, too. Brody came to put his arm under her elbow, and they'd made it up the walk to the first porch step, when he lost his balance. He didn't want them to fall on their backsides on the cement, so he wrenched Harmony sideways, and they both fell into a deep drift of snow.

She landed on top of him, her body stretched over his. Mmm, she kind of liked it here. She stared down at his handsome face, tempted to plaster her lips on his. What would he do? How would he respond?

Ian raced from the house to check on them. Standing on the porch, he called, "Are you all right?"

"Fine, just damned cold." Brody's voice sounded husky. He rolled to his feet and reached to pull Harmony up. His feet slid again, and this time, he fell on top of her. Thankfully, he caught himself on his elbows before he squished her into a pancake.

His gaze locked with hers.

Go ahead. Kiss me. Harmony studied his face, inches from hers. A strong jaw. She was growing fond of those smoky, gray eyes. Full lips. Mmm, the possibilities. But it *was* cold.

"Brody?" Ian waited.

"I'm *fine!*" His voice sounded like ground glass. He rolled to his feet again, and this time, he said, "You might be safer without my help."

Did she want to be safe? Harmony stayed where she was. She flapped her arms up and down and slid her legs back and forth where she lay. "No worries. Just leave me here. I'm a snow angel."

Brody stared at her like she was nuts, then shook his head and started laughing. "Come on, angel, before you become an ice sculpture." He stomped his feet deep into the snow for better footing and carefully pulled her to him. Her body was shaking, and he pushed her slightly away to ask, "Did I hurt you?"

The giggles overwhelmed her. "Only my dignity."

"Very funny." He flicked her nose. "Come on. I'm freezing."

When they reached Ian, he gave them a strange look.

"What?" Brody sounded out of patience.

Ian shrugged. "You can't sue me because you're clumsy."

"I'm not clumsy. I didn't clean the mud off my boots from when I rescued your damned duck, and these boots don't have any treads on the bottom. They're smooth."

"Stick to that story." Ian led them inside the house. "What I saw was a bull in a china shop."

"A bull?" They were bickering when they joined Tessa in the kitchen.

She smiled at all of them and came to hug Brody and Harmony. "Ian told me you were worried about me. You two are so sweet."

Harmony studied her friend. "You still look tired."

"I shouldn't. I took a nap this afternoon. I don't know what happened. I was sitting on the couch, working on my laptop, and the next thing I knew, I woke up two hours later."

"We can order pizza, you know. That's my usual staple." Harmony ignored Brody's grimace.

"Don't be silly. I'm keeping everything low key. I think it's just the weather. I always get tired at the first cold snap. My body has to adjust."

Ian threw an arm around Tessa's shoulders. "Okay, woman, let's eat. Everything's ready."

They marched to the table and took their places. The ribs were delicious. The baked potatoes were on the firm side, but no one said a word. Ian had heated up not one, but two cans of green beans. Perfect.

Ian tried to keep the conversation light. "Brody, you mentioned that Bridget phoned last night, but then Paula called us to lunch, and I forgot to ask you about it. What's up?"

Again, Harmony noticed Brody wince before he said, "Mason wants a puppy, and they're all arguing about it. Her husband's waffling, and that pisses Bridget off. She wanted a firm no from him, so that she doesn't have to be the bad guy."

Ian frowned. "But that's why she loves Dave, because he's so easygoing. He lets her make all the decisions."

Brody's lip curled up on one side. "But she only likes it when it benefits her."

Ian laughed.

Harmony watched Brody. Something was bothering him, she was sure. He was omitting something, but it was not her concern. If he didn't want to share it, there must be a reason.

When the men cleared the table, Ian spread his hands. "I forgot to hoof it to the bakery and thaw something for dessert. Sorry."

"I've had plenty to eat," Harmony said. "I'm going to have to hit the gym and start a diet when I get home."

Brody absently shook his head. "You have a great figure. No worries there."

She could feel the blush creep to her cheeks. Two compliments from Mr. Broody Brody. She wouldn't know what to do with herself. "Thanks, but that's because I'm usually too lazy to fix myself much to eat. I'm constantly getting fed here."

Brody rested a hand on his stomach. "How do you keep the weight off, Ian?"

Ian looked at his wife with a wicked twinkle in his eyes. "I chase Tessa around the house, naked."

Tessa's jaw dropped. A blush crept all the way up to her copper hairline, and she smacked his arm.

Ian laughed at her. "You girls take off. Brody and I will clean up."

Tessa had to push herself out of her chair. Harmony fought to not put a hand under her elbow to help her into the living room.

"You're still dead," Harmony said. "When the guys are done in the kitchen, Brody and I will head back."

"No, we haven't even talked writing!" Tessa pursed her lips in a pout. "Are you getting enough pages done? Will you make your deadline?"

"I'm doing rewrites as I go, and I finished ten new pages today. When I get back, I'll try to squeeze in five more."

"Brody said you're being awfully nice to the kids."

Harmony shrugged. "You've seen me when I get too driven. I use up my brain. It goes dry. The kids give me a nice break. I need it."

Tessa smirked. "You like reading to them."

Harmony couldn't slide a half-truth past Tessa. They'd known each other too long. "Yup, I'm busted. Who knew kids could be so much fun?"

Tessa studied her under lowered lashes. "How do you and Brody get along?"

"Uh-uh, don't go there." Harmony waggled a finger at her friend. "We do okay, but we don't have much in common. We make great houseguests, though."

Tessa smiled and leaned her head back against the high spindles of the rocking chair. Her eyes closed for a second, and she jerked forward, fighting to stay awake.

"Maybe you're catching something." Wasn't it flu season in the Midwest? At home, Harmony usually tried to avoid germy people. For Tessa, she'd brave them to bring her Jell-O and 7-Up. She'd even hold a bucket for her when she puked.

"No fever, no cough, I'm just tired."

"Then take it easy for a while. Hang in there, friend." When Brody came to check on her, Harmony motioned that it was time to leave. He gave a quick nod and said his goodbyes to Ian.

Ian gave them a container of Ice Melt to sprinkle on the cement in front of them as they walked to the SUV. "Try not to kill Harmony on the way to your car. Just leave the container by the driveway. I'll get it in the morning."

On the short trip back to the lodge, Brody concentrated on the road. His car had four-wheel drive, but it was still tense going. He pulled so close to the front door, she only had a few steps before she was in the foyer. Then he parked the SUV and slid across the pavement to join her. Maybe they should keep Ice Melt near his parking place.

When he went to hang his coat on one of the hooks, he fidgeted with it, and then he fidgeted with his boots when he took them off.

She finally asked, "What's the deal? Are you worried about Tessa, too?"

"It's too soon to worry about her," he said. "She might have overdone it before we got here and wiped herself out. She might be catching something. We'll know soon."

"Then what's wrong?" He'd been tense all night.

"I want to ask you something, but I feel stupid."

She waved that away. "Stupid has always appealed to me. Go for it."

He hurried his words. "I don't suppose you'd like to watch the next Harry Potter movie with me? I bought it."

She stared. "Wouldn't that be like cheating? We'd know what happens in the story before I read it to the kids."

"If you think about it, it might help you read better, with more expression. You'll know what to emphasize and what not to."

She couldn't believe it. "That's some of the best rationalization I've heard in a long time. I thought you always did the right thing."

"Most of the time, I try."

"Most of the time?"

He shook his head. "No one's perfect. But I make really good popcorn, and I bought a really nice bottle of wine. Do you like Riesling? I noticed you drink white with Tessa. She thought it might be your favorite."

She kicked off her boots and pushed them close to the wall, under her coat. "You didn't have to try so hard. The popcorn would have done it."

"I could have saved myself fifteen bucks? I'll remember that next time."

"Next time?" She bit her bottom lip to keep from smirking. "You bought all of the movies, didn't you, the whole set?"

"Who else am I going to watch them with? If anybody on my construction crew sees them at my place, I'll never hear the end of it. I'll leave them for the kids when I go home."

She shouldn't. She should write. But it was still early. They hadn't stayed at Ian and Tessa's that long. "I'm game. I like being spoiled. I'll expect wine next time, too."

His eyes glittered, and he looked downright naughty. "That's why I bought a whole case of it."

She slapped her thigh and laughed. "You and I could be great friends!"

He sobered so fast, it surprised her. He blinked and sounded surprised himself. "I would have never guessed—a woman friend who's not a sister." He looked dumb-founded.

She snorted. An unladylike habit. Okay, *another* unladylike habit. "You're thinking too much. I'll help you with the popcorn."

With all their snacks ready, they sat, side by side, on the couch, watching the movie. When the enormous snake in the Chamber of Secrets attacked Harry, Brody's eyes went wide. At the end of the movie, he said, "Isn't that a little scary for kids?"

Harmony fought back a yawn. "What kid doesn't like to be scared?"

He studied her. "You're probably right. It's only when you become an adult that you try to play everything safe. No surprise bumps. Lots of security. Maybe sometimes, we play things too safe."

"Beats me. I just try to keep out of harm's way."

He held her gaze, suddenly thoughtful. "What harmed you? Because something did, didn't it?"

She threw up her hands. "It's too late for deep discussions. Come on. Let's rinse our dirty dishes. I only talked into the wee hours in the morning in my college days."

He chuckled, following her to the kitchen. "Okay, in that case, I'll see you in the morning, but why do I have a feeling you dodge out on deep discussions every chance you get?"

It was her turn to chuckle. "Now you know. I like to play in the shallow end of the pool. And you won't see me in the morning. You'll be happy if I remember to brush my teeth for lunch."

He rinsed the bowls and handed them to her to put in the dishwasher. "You don't take much seriously, but you're a fanatic about your writing. When did you start?"

"When I was young. Writing was always an outlet, an escape, for me." Barricaded in her room, she'd make up happy worlds, full of people she wanted to know. Later, in high school, she discovered urban fantasies. The female protagonists were kick-ass women, self-sufficient. And she knew—that's what she'd be as soon as she moved out on her own.

"When did it become a career?" He leaned against the sink counter, genuinely curious, she could tell.

"It took a while. I worked in a factory during the day and I wrote at night." And through her string of rejection letters, she'd watched the dance of the unfaithful as men and women told their spouses they had to work overtime, so that they could sleep with each other. Her dad had been unfaithful, she was sure. Her mother didn't care, as long as he paid the bills.

What was the point? Why not pay your own bills and be rid of men? She shook off the old memories. "I'd better get some work done before I go to bed. I have five pages to go. See you in the morning."

She could feel the intensity of his gaze on her as she went up the stairs. Poor Brody. He'd never understand her. He'd lived in an orderly world for far too long.

Chapter 8

She finished the last bite of coffee cake at three in the morning. She'd made a half pot of coffee, gotten a second wind, and was so wrapped up in her story that she forgot the time. Her phone sang "Oh, baby, baby . . ." at seven-thirty.

"No." She turned off the alarm and tried to go back to sleep, but Luxar just wouldn't settle down. He pestered her until she stumbled out of bed and returned to her laptop. Seven pages later, she slumped over the desk and fell asleep.

When Brody called at noon to remind her to get ready for lunch, she couldn't remember what day it was. His voice sounded strained. She was a writer. Even when her brain felt fuzzy, she noticed things. Nuances made a big difference in stories. Foreshadowing cranked up tension. Something had been bothering Brody yesterday. It bothered him more today.

A glance out her window confirmed that gray skies and more snow had come to stay. No specks dotted the ice fishing holes today. A wind whipped across the lake and shook the naked branches of the trees in the back yard. She'd remind Brody to clean his boots. Things were going to be even slipperier than before.

When she reached the lobby, a heavy sheet of plastic blocked off the west wing. She lifted it to take a peek. Two-by-fours framed a hallway with four openings for doors. The men had started hanging drywall in the back and must be working their way forward. She could finally picture how the suites would work.

She slid onto her chair at the dining table at exactly twelve thirty, dressed and close to being presentable. She'd even slapped on some mascara and blush. She glanced at the others. Quiet. Gloomy. Delicious-looking sloppy joes and potato chips sat on each plate. No one was paying attention to their food. Paula looked from one brother to the other. Finally, she asked, "Is everything okay?"

Harmony didn't feel right asking, so she was glad Paula did. Tension buzzed in the air. She and Brody were acquaintances, not friends. If he wanted to tell her something, he would, but he hadn't. So it surprised her when he looked directly at her and said, "Cecily's pregnant."

Oh, boy. The woman who wouldn't have his baby had gotten preggo as fast as she could with an older man. "Was it an accident?" she asked.

Brody's mouth went grim. "Not according to my mother. They still bump into each other at social functions. Bridget called to tell me something was up, that Cecily was walking around like . . ." He hesitated.

". . . Her ass weighed a ton?" Harmony finished.

He nodded. "That's how Bridget put it. Bridget would. Mom said Cecily came right up to her to tell her the news and asked her to let me know. Said I'd be happy to hear she finally got knocked up."

"She likes to hurt you." No wonder Brody was so prickly around women.

"When Bridget found out, she started digging around. She knows half of the population in the area."

Ian nodded. "Like Tessa's grandmother. That woman knows everyone."

"She found people who told her the scoop." Brody's broad shoulders hunched. He wasn't happy about the news. "Her husband promised to hire a live-in nanny, so that Cecily wouldn't be tied down. Maybe if I'd thought of that . . ."

"You'd still be hitched to Super Bitch," Ian said.

Harmony felt her eyebrows shoot up. "I thought they only hired nannies in English Regency novels—shuffled the kid off to a nursery and let him visit his parents between social engagements."

Ian shook his head. "No, lots of career women hire nannies so that they can go back to their work or schedules."

Harmony thought about that. Maybe she'd have been better off if her parents had done that. Her dad was a roofer, a "man's man," who loved to hang out with his buddies—golf, bowling, hunting, fishing, tinkering on cars. Her mom worked as a cashier at a dollar store. She loved playing cards and bingo. They spent as little time with Harmony and her brother as possible. There was a roof over her head and always a meal on the table. But she was invisible to them, left to her brother's care.

Brody waited for her to say something. Her lips turned down. She couldn't help it, but her voice sounded more bitter than she intended. "Poor kid, he's going to be pretty much on his own. He's a token baby."

Brody frowned, studying her. "Is that what happened to you?"

The damned man was too perceptive. She shrugged. "My parents provided for me, in their way."

"No siblings?" he asked.

"A brother. I stayed out of his way. He hung out with the wrong people, and he could be mean." She reached over and put her hand on his. "Are you going to be okay? Cecily's pushing out a baby to keep her end of a contract. I hope the father, at least, wants it."

Brody stared at her hand. "He needs an heir, someone to take over his businesses."

Harmony pulled away. Her parents had no expectations for either her or her brother. In some ways, for her, that was a blessing. No pressure. For her brother, it left him feeling adrift. Their parents didn't even notice his bad choices as long as he pretended to meet curfew. "Cecily had better have a boy. Times have changed, but I'm guessing *Mr. Cecily* wants a son."

Brody smiled at her wording. His shoulders relaxed. "I'm okay now. You put it in perspective. Cecily might have a baby, but she still won't be a mother. We still wouldn't have worked."

She tilted her head, studying him. "You hate failure, don't you?"

"I'm getting better at it. I still strive for high standards, but sometimes, your best isn't good enough."

Jeez, is that how he interpreted failure? It made her feel like a slacker. Sometimes *life* happens. She just strove to stay afloat and as pain-free as possible.

As soon as they finished their meal, Brody pushed to his feet. "Come on, Ian. Let's get the hallway finished. Then we can start on the inside walls."

Ian reached to collect their dirty dishes, but Paula waved him away. "I'll get these. You guys look driven today. Pound away."

Appropriate. The hammer gun sounded before Harmony reached the top step. She closed the door on the construction noise and plopped in front of her laptop. She was starting the vast middle of the book. Even with plot points, she struggled with middles. By then, all of the set-up was done. She'd set the plot in motion. Lines were drawn, and she knew who'd step over them. The middle was crunch time, when friendships and enmities deepened, everything got complicated, and she had to wring tension from each and every scene.

She was struggling with a chapter where Luxar went to meet Serifina's coven, and they were all going to join together to fight Torrid and his demons. Luxar didn't trust witches, and witches didn't trust vampires, so everyone was on edge. The dialogue needed to be edgy, sharp. Her writing crawled to a few paragraphs here, a few there, with lots of pacing back and forth between the coffee pot and her laptop. She always drank too much coffee when she wrote tricky scenes. Getting up and down gave her mind time to ponder, turn things over, and try for something fresh. By the time she finished the damned pages, she felt like she was going to float away, she was full of so much liquid. She hurried into the bathroom.

Of course, that's when the kids burst into the room. *Damn.* She'd probably have to cross her legs to finish reading a chapter. When she walked out of the bathroom, she was surprised to see Brody with them.

Chapter 9

Brody gave her a wary glance. "The kids came for me, and Ian wanted to go home to check on Tessa, so I tagged along. Can I stay, too?"

He sounded like a kid. That made it easier for her to say yes.

Bailey had a firm grip on his hand. She didn't intend to let go. Harmony smiled. Brody had been whipped by a five-year-old, and who could blame him?

Harmony shrugged and headed to the easy chair in the corner. "Just bring your library manners."

She shook her head. Where had that come from? A blast from the past. When she was little, she walked eight blocks to the library every Saturday morning to hear one of the librarians read to kids. Then she'd check out the three-book limit she was allowed to take home and read during the week. She'd done that for months until her brother made fun of her for being a book nerd. That wouldn't have stopped her, but when he grabbed the top book on her pile and ripped the pages out of it, she knew she was beat. Her parents paid for the book, but told her *no more.*

"Your brother's embarrassed with all of your reading. Give it a rest."

It had pissed her off, but she was ten. If she'd had magical powers like Serifina, she'd have turned them all into toads. But she didn't. So she started watching Saturday morning cartoons instead.

She looked up to see Brody studying her. "A penny for your thoughts."

She shrugged. "Made me think of the librarian who read to us every Saturday when I was a kid."

His look said he knew there was more, but he didn't push it. Instead, he settled in the chair beside hers and lifted Bailey onto his lap. Aiden, as usual, flopped on the unmade bed. Harmony grimaced. 'I'd have made it if I'd known you were coming."

Brody gave it a glance. "Why?"

"You like things neat."

"Then *I* should make the bed." He leaned back and got comfortable.

Harmony decided it was safer to start reading the book.

Aiden couldn't stand it when she reached the part where Harry had to promise to stay in his room and not make a noise for the third time. "Why are they so mean to him?" he demanded.

"Did they want Harry?" Harmony asked.

"No."

"Do they like magic?"

"No, but that's silly!" Aiden cried.

"Why do you think they hate magic so much?"

They debated that for a few minutes, and Harmony loved how quick Aiden jumped from one idea to the next. He thought about cause and effect, motivation, and emotions. Then she glanced at the clock. "We'd better read some more."

When she reached the place where Harry looked at the hedge and green eyes stared back at him, Aiden could hardly stand it. "Who's hiding in there?"

Harmony shrugged. "I haven't read any further than you have." True enough, but she and Brody had watched the movie. Shame on them.

At the end of the chapter, Aiden begged her to read a few more pages. "You can't stop there!" he cried. "We have to know who's sitting on Harry's bed."

She looked at the clock. "We have fifteen more minutes . . ."

"Go for it," Brody said.

She looked at him, surprised.

"Inquiring minds." He smiled.

She started the next chapter.

Aiden squirmed with excitement when they met Dobby. He wiggled in fear when Dobby kept making noise in Harry's room. "He's going to get Harry in trouble."

"Yup, looks that way," Harmony said. At five thirty, she quit reading. "That's it for the day, kiddos. Scram."

Aiden hesitated. "Did you ever want to write stories for kids?"

"Hell, no." She pinched her lips together. Where were her manners? "I don't have any kids, wouldn't know where to start."

Aiden frowned. "But you were a kid once. You have to remember."

"Not so much. Besides, I was a rotten kid. Got in trouble a lot."

"Really?" He studied her. She must not look like a troublemaker to him. "For what?"

Harmony shrugged. "Couldn't concentrate in school. My mind was always wandering off. My teachers got sick of me. I spent a lot of time writing words from the dictionary in the principal's office."

Bailey laughed. "I get all As at school."

"That's because you're a smart, little girl. Your mom's probably really proud of you."

Aiden was still curious. "Did you have any brothers and sisters?"

"One brother, older than me. He didn't like me all that much. It was mutual."

Aiden stared. "But you were his little sister." He put an arm around Bailey.

Harmony shrugged. "We didn't have anything common." She pointed at the clock. "Five forty. Again."

Aiden grabbed Bailey's hand, who grabbed Brody's hand, and they set off.

"See you in a minute," Brody called back to her.

She nodded and hustled into the bathroom. Her blush had melted. She looked washed out. She always did in January. By February, her complexion would look like a sallow zombie's and she'd wince every time she saw her own reflection. She smeared on some foundation and dabbed on more blush.

Brody was sitting in the SUV, waiting for her, when she reached the foyer. She scurried out and got in. Once again, they crept down the treacherous road to Tessa's house. Surely someday, the county would salt and sand this street? In her city, mayors won and lost elections on how well streets were cleared in winters.

Brody's frown turned fierce as he drove. Maybe tomorrow, he'd call and complain to some county official. But then he surprised her by saying, "I can't believe no one's ever told Aiden to shut up when he's around adults. I didn't think the kid would ever stop asking questions while you read."

Harmony whipped her head to see him better. Her hands curled into fists. "I encouraged him to talk about the story. I like how much he questions things. Only really smart kids . . ."

Her words died on her lips. A huge, *gotcha* grin had spread across Brody's face. "You like kids more than you let on."

Chin up, voice chilly, she said, "It's not nice to play devil's advocate. Didn't your mother teach you that?"

"She might have mentioned it."

She let out an exasperated sigh. "No wonder your sisters gave you a hard time."

"They'd have given me a hard time no matter what I did. Wait till you meet them."

Harmony pressed a hand to her chest. She did everything humanly possible to avoid family get-togethers. They brought back too many bad memories. The annual, summer reunion her parents dragged them to always started with laughing and drinking and ended with shouting and recriminations. "Are they coming to visit Ian, too?"

"No, no, I didn't mean to startle you. I just meant, *if* you ever meet them. You're one of Tessa's best friends. I suppose it's possible in the future."

"Not if I can help it." She saw his expression—a little offended. "That didn't come out right, but I try to avoid big groups. *Any* big groups. I enjoy having a few friends over instead."

"You survive conferences."

"That's different." How could she explain? "I'm on panels. We talk business, writing. It's things I'm comfortable with."

"And you don't think you'd be comfortable with my sisters?"

She frowned at him. They were inching down the highway. They'd be late for sure. "I doubt your sisters talk writing. They probably talk about mutual friends and their kids and family—stuff I'm not good at."

"I see." What the hell did that mean? And what difference did it make? He pulled into Ian's drive and sighed with relief. "The sidewalk looks safe."

Harmony shook her head, confused. She reached for the door handle, but he asked another question.

"Your childhood wasn't all that great, was it?"

"No, but it wasn't all that bad either." She knew people who'd had it far, far worse.

He nodded, and they got out of the car and headed to the house.

Tessa greeted them. "Ian's grilling steaks on the back patio. Supper will be ready in a few minutes."

Harmony studied her as she led them into the kitchen. Her frizzy, copper hair was flat. A no shower day, for sure. Her creamy complexion looked pale. "Are you okay?"

Right then, Ian came in the back door, teeth chattering. His nose and cheeks glowed like Rudolph's. He held a platter with four steaks, tented in foil.

Tessa looked embarrassed. "I baked with Grandma all morning. I felt great. I wanted to make bouillabaisse, but the smells bothered me. I kept getting nauseous."

"Oh, shit." Brody shook his head.

Ian frowned at him.

"You need to go see a doctor," Brody said.

"What do you think is wrong with her?" Ian sounded concerned.

"I don't think I'm sick," Tessa said. "Or contagious."

"Neither do I." Brody went to the refrigerator to fetch two beers. "I think you'd better start taking prenatal vitamins."

Ian stared. So did Tessa and Harmony.

Tessa asked, "What do you mean?"

Brody raised an eyebrow. "I think you'd better pee on a stick."

Ian's expression flashed with revelation. "Oh, no, not like Maeve."

"Puked her brains out every morning for weeks," Brody said.

"Morning sickness?" Harmony gazed at her friend.

Brody popped the cap off his beer bottle and took a swig. "Go buy a pregnancy test at the drugstore. They're accurate."

Ian's brown eyes went wide, and Tessa reached out a hand to grip the countertop. Clearly she needed to brace herself.

Ian grabbed Brody's shoulder. "Let's go."

"Do you know how bad the roads are?"

"So drive slow. I have to know."

Brody shook his head. "Not until I get my steak."

"It'll wait. Tess'll put it in a warm oven." Ian grabbed a handful of Brody's sweater and started for the door.

Tessa began pacing. She kept mumbling to herself. Harmony tried to calm her, but never found the right thing to say.

A half hour later, the men were back. Tessa disappeared into the bathroom, then opened the door so Ian could watch the strip with her.

When it turned blue, Ian whooped with joy. Tessa grabbed ahold of the doorframe.

"Do you need a bucket?" Harmony asked. Tessa looked like she might be sick again.

Ian pulled her to him. "It's going to be okay, babe. We're going to make great parents."

"But we were going to wait a year . . ."

Ian cut off her worries. "So what? The universe sent us a surprise. An awesome one."

When they sat down to eat, Tessa's hands shook. Harmony thought she might have to offer to cut her steak into bite-sized pieces for her. Ian looked like he'd explode if he couldn't shout his news to the world sometime soon.

Tessa was so shaken, Harmony reached for her hand. "Did you use protection?"

"All but one time. We were in . . . sort of a rush."

Ian smirked. "Things got a little out of control."

"But you want kids?" Harmony persisted.

"Oh, yes. We were going to wait a year, to give ourselves some time as a couple. But I'm twenty-eight." Tessa stared at her, eyes wide. "You need to think about that. You're older than I am. If you don't get to it pretty soon, time's running out."

Harmony grimaced. "Thanks for making me feel ancient." Brody laughed, and she glared at him. "Men don't have to worry as much, but it's different for women."

"So you *do* want kids?" Brody said.

"Hell no, it's just that I know I'm making a choice. My option's running out."

Brody glanced at Ian, confused. Ian just shrugged and said, "Women."

"What have you got against kids?" Brody asked. "You like Aiden and Bailey."

"They're not mine. I read to them, then send them downstairs to their mom. Kids suck the life out of you. My friends were fun to hang out with until they had kids. Now they collapse around ten at night. They barely keep up with their rug rats."

"What are you saying? That I'm not going to be fun anymore?" Tessa pushed the food on her plate from one spot to another. No one was eating.

Harmony sighed. "I'm just saying that kids change everything. I'll still love hanging out with you, Tessie, but I'm not ready for that kind of a commitment."

Brody shook his head. "The parents I've talked to wouldn't change anything. The kids are worth it."

Harmony pointed a finger at Mr. Know-It-All. "Then you'd better get busy. You're forty. If you don't find a girl and start popping out babies soon, you'll be an old man in diapers before your last kid graduates from college."

Brody jerked back in his chair and stared at her, surprised. No, maybe shocked. He swallowed, hard. "You have a unique way of putting things, but you're right. I don't want to roll up in a wheelchair to watch my grandkids play Little League."

She hadn't meant to rattle him, but she had an awful feeling she had. She tried to put it more mildly. "You'd better start looking."

"You're right, damn it. It's time I get back in the game." He raised a dark eyebrow. "You'd make someone a great wife. You don't think so, but you're generous with your time and emotions. You shouldn't rule out being June Cleaver."

Tessa laughed and tried to cover it by pretending to cough.

Harmony snorted. "Yeah, that's me—all warm and fuzzy in an apron and pearls while I vacuum." She looked down at her steak. She watched Brody saw through his. Somewhere between trying to thaw them in a rush and keep them warm in the oven, they'd turned to leather. Ian was fidgeting too much to eat, and Tessa looked done in. She sighed. "What if we call it an early night? You guys would prob-ably like to talk."

Brody put down his fork and stood before Ian could answer. "You need some couple time. We'll help you clean up, then take off."

Ian and Tessa didn't argue, so they all pitched in, and in a short while, Brody and Harmony zipped to his SUV. The road had been sanded and salted sometime during their visit. It still wasn't easy going. It took them a while to reach the lodge, but it wasn't the white-knuckle drive it usually was. Harmony waited in the foyer for Brody, and when he came in, he asked, "Are you as hungry as I am?"

She pressed a hand to her stomach. "I'm starving."

They headed to the kitchen and scrounged for food. Lots of eggs and some ham slices and lots of cheese, but they weren't sure what

Paula needed for breakfast and lunch tomorrow, so they ended up making a stack of peanut butter sandwiches and popcorn.

Brody looked at her. "The next Harry Potter?"

She poured herself a glass of wine, and he grabbed a beer. They carried all of their goodies to the library. They were snacking and watching the movie when Aiden stuck his head around the door.

Brody frowned. "Why aren't you in bed? You have school tomorrow."

"I keep having nightmares, can't sleep. Can I stay with you a while?"

Harmony scooted closer to Brody on the sofa, and Aiden came to press himself against her side. "Does your mother know?"

Paula answered from the doorway. She looked dead on her feet. "He's been having a few rough nights. Come on, kiddo, you can sleep in my bed."

Aiden shook his head, snuggling closer to Harmony. "You're watching Harry Potter." Oops, busted. But he was too tired to be upset. "Can I watch a while?"

Paula looked at Harmony. Harmony glanced at the boy. He looked nervous, afraid. She shrugged. "Hell, why not?" The kid could hardly keep his eyes open. Maybe he just needed something to jostle his thoughts away from whatever was bothering him.

"When your movie's over, I'll leave the door unlocked, and you can bring him into our apartment and let him sleep on the couch. I'll put his pillow and blanket there." Before she left, Paula looked at them and mouthed the words *thank you.*

Brody hit the play button on the movie, and half an hour later, Aiden was asleep. Brody nodded toward him. "I can carry him to Paula's couch, so you don't have to keep holding him."

Harmony ran her fingers through the boy's soft hair. "He's no bother. Let him reach deep sleep, then he might not dream anymore tonight. Poor kid, something's eating at him."

When the movie ended, Brody gently lifted him, and Harmony went with him to settle Aiden on Paula's couch. They gazed down at him. "He looked scared to me," Brody said.

Harmony nodded. "I used to have nightmares when my brother threatened to beat me up. He hated it when my parents made him stay home with me when they went out."

Brody's expression turned grim. "What's your brother doing now?"

"He moved to Texas. I think he's a trucker, but he changes jobs a lot."

Brody shook his head. He was damned good-looking when he brooded. His gaze settled on Aiden. "If he sees war scenes on the evening news, do you think he dreams about his dad? That has to be tough for a kid."

Harmony pressed her lips together. "I sure as hell hope not."

When they left Paula's apartment, they gathered their dirty dishes and carried them to the kitchen. Tonight, they plopped at the work-table and Brody drank another beer and she had another glass of wine.

This time, Brody made silly small talk. He told stories about when he and Ian were little boys and how their sisters used to dress Ian up in strange costumes when they had tea parties. He told her how he and Ian had decided to sneak out of the house and had crawled out on the porch roof, then made it to the big tree and started down it when their mother shone a flashlight on them and threatened to wake their dad. By the time they glanced at the clock and decided they'd better call it a night, Harmony was relaxed and happy. When she climbed the stairs to her room, she realized Brody was every bit as appealing when he was being silly as when he was brooding and serious.

She stared at her laptop. She was too tired to write tonight. She set her alarm for six-thirty to get an early start in the morning.

Chapter 10

Harmony jumped out of bed at six-thirty with all kinds of ideas for her new scene flying in her head. Bless the good, old subconscious. It always worked overtime, especially if she wasn't watching. She grabbed coffee, took the last slice of coffee cake—a little on the stale side now—and hit the laptop's keys. Things between Luxar and Serifina were heating up. Battles were brewing. By the time she went downstairs for lunch, she was beaming.

Brody and Ian were still pounding on something in the west wing. Another wall must be going up. She looked in the cream-colored dining room, but didn't see Paula. She glanced at her watch. Hmm, everyone must be late this time except her. She grabbed a magazine and snuggled down on a soft, leather sofa in the lobby to wait for them. When the pounding stopped, and Brody walked out and saw her, he glared. "Did you swallow a canary? You look awfully damned pleased with yourself today."

She laughed at his foul mood. "Someone must not have had a good morning, but I was on time. You weren't."

Ian came up behind him. "We hit a snag, building a closet."

"Life happens." She stood and looked around. Were they skipping lunch today and no one told her? "Are you always this grumpy when things don't go your way?" she asked Brody.

He scowled. "I had a hell of a time sleeping last night, kept thinking about things." The scowl darkened. "It was your fault."

"My fault?" What had she done?

"You and your comment about me getting too old to have kids." He narrowed his eyes at her . . . considering. It made her nervous.

She waved him off. "You're not going to ruin my mood. I got up early and have fifteen pages written today—already! And they're good ones."

Brody thought about that as Ian motioned them toward the kitchen. "How many do you usually write?"

"I'm not a fast writer. I'm lucky when I get eight decent pages. I always do my rewrites in the morning before I start the new stuff."

Ian nodded. "That's about what Tessa writes, too. She says if she gets ten pages a day, then in thirty days of writing, she'll have a rough draft. She doesn't write on weekends. Has the bakery to run on Friday and Saturday mornings."

Brody scratched his head. Sawdust fell to his shoulder. He grimaced and scrubbed his hands through his hair, shaking out the rest. "A lot more goes into writing than I thought."

"Why would you think about it? Only writers fiddle with that kind of stuff." Harmony looked around and frowned. "Where's Paula?"

Ian finished herding them into the kitchen. "She made sandwiches and a salad for us, but then took hers to the apartment to eat. Aiden's home from school today, sick. Paula thinks he's faking, but he's never pulled this before, so she doesn't know what's up."

"Something's bothering him." Harmony's mouth set in a firm line. She glanced at Brody, and he nodded.

"We'll figure it out." He looked at his brother. "How's Tessa today?"

"She doesn't get sick when she eats, but she loses it when she cooks and the smells hit her. I'm sorry, but I think we're going to have to eat at the diner for a while."

Brody's expression turned to calculating. A worry wriggled down Harmony's spine. He tossed an arm over her shoulders, as if they were comrades. At first, it surprised her, but then heat replaced her worry. "No need to. If you let Harmony and me use the kitchen here, we'll cook dinners and bring them to your place. That way, no cooking smells, just food."

Ian stared. "What made you think of that?"

Harmony stared, too. What the hell was he thinking? Did he hate eating out that much? She needed to get fifteen pages written a day! She was already stopping every afternoon to read to kids. Now he wanted her to cook?

"Harmony volunteered for us to come to your place and help Tessa cook, remember? We'll just take it one step farther."

Okay, she *had* volunteered to do that. Tessa was her best friend. She'd pitch in to help if Tessa needed it. If they could cook something fast, before they went to the bungalow, that was doable.

Ian crossed his arms over his chest, unimpressed. "You don't know how to cook."

Brody grimaced. He obviously couldn't argue that point. "True, but Harmony does."

Ian shook his head. He didn't trust Brody's offer. Neither did Harmony.

Brody gave her shoulders a squeeze. "Harmony and I both love Tessa. Tell us what her favorites are, and we'll make them."

What? He was getting a little overconfident now. "But I only know . . ."

Brody interrupted her. "If you can make a dozen killer dishes, you can make lots more. We'll look for recipes online."

Ian eyed his brother with suspicion. "Okay, I'll call your bluff. This should be interesting."

Harmony gulped. What had just happened?

"We can talk about it over lunch." Ian settled at the kitchen worktable where Paula had left a plate full of toasted, ham and cheese sandwiches. Feeling dazed, Harmony reached for one. After peanut butter sandwiches for supper last night, she was salivating. She raised an eyebrow at Brody when he took two, then she glanced at the gleaming, stainless steel appliances. Somehow, they seemed more intimidating than her battered white stove and refrigerator at home.

"Do you do any cooking at all?" she asked him.

"I reheat things really well." His bite took a fourth of the sandwich.

She frowned at him. The man looked smug. She got the feeling she was missing something, but couldn't decide what it might be.

"I'll make a great sous chef," he guaranteed her.

She heaved a sigh. "This might push my limits. I can't compete with Tessa, but we can come up with something." She turned a worried look on Ian. "What about her baking?"

"That doesn't bother her. She thinks it's the smell of grease and meat that make her queasy." He was studying his brother.

Brody shrugged. "Harmony and I can handle meat."

"Since when? I've seen you grill, but this isn't exactly grill season." The brothers locked gazes, some kind of silent communication passing between them, and suddenly, Ian blinked, surprised. He grinned from ear to ear. "You guys are the best! Harmony will need lots of help. Tessa loves soups and casseroles. You don't have to make anything fancy."

Harmony looked back and forth between them. What was with the sudden mood swing? Now they *both* looked too innocent. Oh, crikey! She was doomed.

"One-pot meals are a good idea." Brody nodded. "That way, Tessa'll have leftovers for lunch."

Why did Harmony feel like she was being steamrolled? She looked at the two men, sure she was missing something, but they gazed back at her with their polite expressions. That worried her even more. They must have given their poor mother fits when they were growing up. What were they up to? She pursed her lips, wary, but why not cook for Tessa?

She decided to give in graciously. "I make a killer potato soup. One of my friends is allergic to milk and I make it with coconut milk, chicken broth, and a pinch of curry powder."

Ian looked worried. "I don't think we have coconut milk in the pantry."

"No problem." Brody had an answer for everything. "Harmony and I will come up with menus, then drive into town and stock up enough for a couple of weeks." When Harmony looked startled, he hurried to add, "The food will be on me as a baby present for both of you. It'll be fun to go shopping together, right?"

Fun? Was he nuts? Did he have any idea how long it would take?

Ian's brown eyes glittered with amusement. "You're going to buy our food *and* cook it?"

Brody looked like he might throttle his little brother. "Do you have a problem with that?"

"No. *No!* It's great. Remember. Nothing too spicy."

Brody nodded and started for the door. "I'll get my laptop."

Harmony blinked. "Right now?"

"We need something for supper, right?" He looked to Ian for confirmation.

When Ian nodded, he turned to Harmony. "Is that okay with you? I guess I could grab something from the diner to bring back for tonight."

She rubbed her forehead, befuddled. Everything was moving so quickly, she hardly had time to think. "No, we might as well do it now. I met my page quota for the day. If I lose this afternoon, I'm all right."

"Okay then." Brody hurried out of the room before she could change her mind. For a big man, he could move awfully fast. He called back to Ian, "You can paint the first suite without me, can't you?"

Ian nodded. "Luther's coming to help. He's happy to make a little overtime money."

Harmony remembered. "His wife just had a baby, didn't she?" Tessa was especially fond of Luther and his girlfriend. No, make that new wife. Good grief, were the planets aligned somehow so that women were more fertile and horny than usual? There seemed to be a trend lately.

Ian grinned. "You should see their baby. A little girl. She couldn't be cuter."

Footsteps crossed the front lobby, and Luther popped his head around the kitchen door—a kid—maybe eighteen or nineteen—with dirty-blonde hair and a wiry build. Harmony couldn't imagine having a baby when she was his age. But Tessa had told her that he could hardly keep his hands off his new daughter. When he saw her, he almost backed away, but Ian held up a hand. "I'm coming. Just let me rinse our dishes." A second later, Ian disappeared to paint with Luther.

Brody returned in a few minutes with his laptop. Harmony sat down next to him, and he moved his stool even closer, so she could see. They bumped shoulders as he scrolled through recipes. At first, Harmony felt crowded. Then she relaxed and let herself enjoy his proximity. Strength rolled off him. He seemed to be enjoying their nearness, too, the way he bent in.

Brody made a list—Friday: potato soup, Saturday: pork roast with veggies in a slow cooker, Sunday: beef and noodles, then chicken pot pie, Manhattan clam chowder, shepherd's pie, and chicken enchiladas. All things she could make.

"One week, done." Talk about efficient. They had menus and grocery items. He turned a dazzling smile on her. The man could be charming when he put his mind to it.

They came up with food for a second week and listed every new ingredient they needed on the grocery list. He was nothing but thorough. When they finished, Brody printed everything out in Ian's office and gave a satisfied sigh. "What do you think? Ian and Tessa will have plenty of leftovers and not one thing that's too spicy."

Harmony shook her head. She'd never planned this much in her life. It looked like enough food to feed an army, but if it made Brody happy, why not? She couldn't imagine how much money it would cost, but that didn't seem to bother him. She broached the subject, "This is going to get expensive."

He stared. "We don't have anything extravagant on it, no steak or lobster or seafood."

"No, but you're buying a lot, all at one time."

"Oh, that." He shrugged. "We have to eat, right?"

"I guess."

He grabbed her arm and gave her a quick hug. "We'll be a team. I bet we'll work well together. If we hurry, we can make it to the store and back before the kids come up for you to read to them."

The kids? Harmony had forgotten. She glanced at the clock. "We have three hours."

"Get your coat." Brody was already on his way to the door.

Harmony sighed and followed him. Once Brody made a decision, he acted on it. That much was obvious.

Chapter 11

The roads had been treated, and the drive into Mill Pond wasn't too bad. The town itself was small with quaint brick buildings lining Main Street. They passed the diner and found the grocery store at the other end of the business district.

"What if I push the cart and pay, and you choose what we need?" Brody looked slightly lost, and Harmony suspected he'd never done serious food shopping before. They wandered the aisles for over an hour, filling the cart with everything on Brody's list. Harmony started to wonder if the cart would hold everything.

Every time someone stopped Brody to say *hi*, he made a point of wrapping his arm around her waist and introducing her. Not a bad thing. Her body tingled every time he pressed her close to his side. But once she left Mill Pond, she'd never see these people again. He was stretching good manners further than necessary. Brody was an old-school type of person, though. He stuck to protocol.

An attractive, young woman with a short Afro and a stunning, heart-shaped face stopped him in aisle three. Her dark eyes danced with curiosity. "We heard you were back in town, helping Ian at his place."

Brody reached for Harmony's hand to introduce her. "Harmony, Darinda. Darinda's one of Tessa's oldest friends. Darinda, Harmony— one of Tessa's writer friends."

"Tessa's told me about you, girl." Darinda noticed the hand thing, and her full lips curled in delight. "Spill, Brody. Are you two an item? I thought you'd sworn off women after your divorce."

An item? Embarrassed, Harmony pulled her hand away. Shaking her head, she said, "We're just shopping so we can cook for Tessa a while."

"That's so sweet of you!" Darinda glowed with excitement. "I can't believe my BFF's gonna have a baby."

"Does everyone know?" Brody inched closer to Harmony, and she glanced up at him. Did Darinda make him nervous? He didn't look nervous. It would be hard to shake Brody. Had she hit on him the last time he visited here, and he was warning her off? No, Darinda was happily married. Tessa talked about her husband and kids, what a neat family they were.

Darinda rolled her eyes. "This is Mill Pond, sweetie. There are no secrets here. Grams has been spreading the word."

Brody grinned. "I've heard about Grams."

Darinda threw her arms around him in a quick hug. "Baby, you're gonna be an uncle soon. You won't be able to stay away from Mill Pond. We'll see more of you." She left them to their burgeoning cart, and Brody kept adding things they didn't need. Harmony kept complaining, but her words fell on deaf ears.

"Do you like chocolate? Should we buy some of that? What about wine? What's your favorite?" Brody acted like the proverbial kid in a candy shop.

She finally stopped, hands on hips, and demanded, "When was the last time you were in a store?"

He shook his head. "I don't remember. This is great, isn't it?"

"Your bill's going to be horrible."

He shrugged. "A vacation would cost a lot more, and it wouldn't be half as much fun."

"Really? This is your idea of a good time? Where the hell do you go when you want to get away?"

He grinned. "This is a different kind of fun."

She knew he was rich, but her middle-class mind could hardly wrap itself around busting a budget like this. When she finally got him out of the store, he reached for her hand again on the ride home. He was sure in a touchy-feely mood today. As usual, though, he woke up her hormones. What girl could resist such blatant masculinity?

He patted her hand, then pulled away to place his on the steering wheel. "Thanks for this. I think the world of Tessa, and this is something we can do to help her."

How could she argue with that? Mr. Responsible had a big heart. When they turned into the resort's drive, Brody called Ian and Luther to help them carry everything into the lodge. Luther stared at the army of bags in awe. Ian's eyebrows rose. He looked at Harmony.

She grumbled, "Don't ask."

Ian grinned. "Next time, I get to go with you. Tessa never lets me buy everything I want."

"Harmony's no better. She kept telling me no."

Ian gaped at the bags. "Then I don't even want to know what you thought you needed to buy."

It took a while to put everything away. When they finished, Harmony found a huge, deep pot to start making the soup. She whipped into work mode, and Brody faithfully chopped onions, carrots, and celery to sauté. While he cut chunks of potatoes, she added the chicken broth and seasonings. They barely finished in time.

"Should we put the soup in the refrigerator?" Brody asked.

Harmony shook her head. "No, we're taking it to Tessa's in an hour. It'll be fine."

The kids saw them walk out of the kitchen and came to traipse up the stairs with them. On the way, Brody studied Aiden. "Are you feeling better now?"

Aiden nodded, but looked nervous.

"Are you doing all right with your classes at school?" Harmony asked. "Are you worried about your grades?"

Aiden gave her a look. "School's easy."

Brody tried next. "Do you like your teacher?"

He got a dreamy look on his face. "Miss Fredericks is great."

Harmony smiled. He had a crush on her. When they reached her room and settled into their chairs, and Aiden flopped on the bed, she said, "Then what's the deal? Why did you skip today?"

"A mean kid's picking on him," Bailey blurted.

Aiden gave her a dirty look. "Shut up!"

Brody's shoulders squared. He glowered. "Like calling you names or hitting you?"

Aiden pulled up the sleeve of his shirt and showed them a big bruise. "Mom told me to tell my teacher about it. I don't want to, but Mom says Dirk won't stop if I don't."

Brody nodded. "Your mom's right. Bullies enjoy hurting people, and they keep doing it until someone makes them quit."

Aiden frowned at him. "Did anyone ever pick on you?"

Harmony couldn't imagine anyone picking on Brody. First, he was big. Secondly, he had an attitude. He'd fight back, even if he lost.

Brody shook his head. "No one bothered me or Ian. Ian was too antsy, too mouthy. No one wanted to find out what would happen if he got riled."

"Even you?" Bailey asked.

Brody looked surprised. "He was too smart for that, but he found ways to bug me. Bridget had a terrible temper, and that scared people away, but some mean girls picked on Maeve."

"What happened?" Aiden glanced at Bailey, worried.

"I was in high school, and she was in middle school, but Ian took care of it."

Harmony was almost afraid to ask, but couldn't stop herself. She was too nosey. "What did he do?"

"He left presents for each of them in their lockers."

Bailey bit her bottom lip. "What kinds of presents?"

"Garter snakes, black racers, a few corn snakes. Girls scream a lot around those."

Harmony burst out laughing.

Brody grinned. "He let it be known he could find other things. He hinted he knew where a skunk had a den."

Aiden said, "I'd get in trouble if I took a snake to school."

"Ian did, too, but he didn't seem to mind. The girls left Maeve alone after that."

Harmony patted Aiden's head. "Your teacher will know what to do. Your mom gave you good advice. Talk to Miss Fredericks. She'll help you."

Aiden was more subdued when they read the new chapter, and he was quiet when he and Bailey followed Brody downstairs to their apartment.

Brody glanced back at her. "I'll load the soup in the SUV and meet you at the door."

A cue for her to hustle. The man was getting a little too damned demanding, but she glanced at the clock and sped up. Ten minutes later, she climbed into his warm vehicle. He gave her a sheepish look. Harmony's heart did a funny twist. How could she stay irritated with him when he looked repentant? Repentant for what, though?

He cleared his throat. "I need to apologize. I bulldozed you today, and you lost all of your writing time. That's what you came here to do. I'm sorry."

She stared. How could one man disrupt her routine so much and then manage to make her feel fine about it? She shook her head. A contrite Brody was hard to resist. "You're on a time schedule, too," she said. "You gave up your work time to help Tessa. So can I."

His smile came too readily, and a tiny part of her wondered if she was being played. No, this was Brody. He was too intense, too moody to be that sneaky. Wasn't he? On the drive to Tessa's, she decided that she'd better be more cautious around this man. He might be cleverer than he looked.

Chapter 12

When Brody carried the pot of soup into Tessa's kitchen, all of Harmony's reservations fled. Her friend looked so relieved, Harmony knew Brody had made the right choice. Tessa could use a little TLC right now. Brody sat the pot on the stove, and they carried their bowls over to dish up. Ian put crackers on the table and an apple pie, baked fresh that morning from Tessa's bakery.

Brody shifted spots at the table, sitting next to Harmony, so that she could look across at Tessa. When he tasted the soup, he sighed. "You're right, Harm, your recipe is killer."

She raised an eyebrow. "Harm?"

He shrugged. "What in the hell is a nickname for Harmony? Harmy? Mony? What did kids at school call you?"

"*No one* would call me that anymore and live."

He laughed. "What's your last name? Does anyone call you that?"

She glared. "What's the deal with a nickname? Is your tongue too tired to say three syllables?"

"No, but we're friends now. Ian calls Tessa *Tess*. I should have something to call you."

"I haven't started calling you Bro, have I?" She reached for more crackers.

He grimaced. "That doesn't sound very endearing. Not like true friends." He brightened. "Our last name's McGregor. You could call me Mac."

"Or she could call you Knucklehead," Ian offered.

Brody turned to Tessa for help. "What do you call Ian?"

She smiled. "Just plain Ian. Some names don't translate well into nicknames."

He sighed. "Okay, I get it. Harmony, it is."

Harmony bumped his shoulder with her own. "My last name's Meyer. Will that work?"

He considered it and shook his head. "Nope, I don't like that."

"Why not?" She stood to get a refill on her soup, took his empty bowl with her, to get him more, too.

"Someday, when you marry, it won't apply."

"Like that's gonna happen." She ladled soup into their bowls.

"You never know, and then I'd lose my nickname for you." He took his bowl from her, crunched a handful of crackers, and dropped them in.

Harmony shook her head. "I guess you're destined to be frustrated then."

"Looks like it." But she could tell his mind was still turning the problem over, and she dreaded what he'd come up with. *Harm* was bad enough.

She turned to Tessa. "How was baking this morning?"

"Fine, I love working with Grandma, but by the time we finished, I was ready for a nap."

"Are you okay with being a mom now?" she asked.

Tessa's face lit up. "More than okay, I can't wait. I'm going to have to beat Grandma away, though. She and Miguel are already volunteering to babysit on weekends."

Harmony laughed. Tessa had told her about her grandma hinting for a new baby in the family.

When they finished their soup, Brody carried the bowls to the sink, rinsed them, and put them in the dishwasher while Ian cut slices of pie. The three of them drank coffee with their dessert, but Tessa declined. "No use pushing my luck," she said.

They ate on paper plates and threw them away. The rest of the cleanup went quickly, and Brody and Harmony were walking out the door at eight thirty.

Once they were on the road, Brody frowned at her. "I suppose this is going to prove your theory that once a woman's pregnant, she's no fun anymore."

Harmony blinked at him. "Tessa will always be fun, no matter what."

"But you wouldn't be?"

"I'm not fun now. If I'm grouchy during good times, why would a baby change that?"

He hesitated with his answer, slowing down gradually to give himself plenty of time to make the turn into the lodge's drive. The temperatures had dropped, and the roads were a little slippery again. He pulled to the front door and glanced at her. "I think you're fun."

She snorted. "You're as grouchy as I am. What would you know?"

In the dim light, she watched him blink in surprise before he burst out laughing. "You might be right. Frivolous people get on my nerves."

"You wouldn't like a little Miss Sunshine, who hummed in the kitchen and fetched your slippers?"

"God, no."

She grinned at him. "See? I've been good for you. You know what to rule out now in your wife search."

"I'll keep that in mind."

She hurried into the foyer, then waited for him, like usual, but he looked as tired as she felt when he trudged across the resort's parking lot to join her. He stifled a yawn.

"I'm sorry. I don't think I can do a movie tonight," he said.

She sighed with relief. "Good, because I'd fall asleep on you."

"Really?" He gave her a look that could curl toes. "Do you snore in your sleep?"

She laughed. "Probably, but be warned. If you fall asleep first, I get to prank you."

That caught his attention. "What would you do, draw a Sharpie mustache on my upper lip?"

"Nothing that nice. I'd make smiley faces around both of your nipples."

"You'd have to unbutton my shirt to do that. Are you brave enough?"

"I've seen men's bare chests before."

"The voice of experience." He bent down and kissed her forehead. "Sweet dreams, Harm. Sorry I messed up your day."

"You're back to Harm? Really?"

"A woman who draws on men's nipples gets what she deserves."

She smiled. She'd brought that on herself. On the way up the stairs, she gently touched a finger to where his lips smooched her skin. Nice. She wouldn't wash her face there tonight. As she drifted off to sleep, her thoughts turned to Luxar and Serifina.

Ooh, they were getting naughty. Luxar had made it past first base, but Serifina pulled away, not ready to make a full commitment yet. And that's when Harmony realized that once again, Luxar looked exactly like Brody.

Chapter 13

Harmony slept in the next morning. She always let herself have slow starts on weekends. Aiden had told her they couldn't read with her. Their mom liked spending time with them when they were out of school. That worked for her. She liked to goof off on Saturday mornings and eat lunch before she hit the keys.

She got showered and dressed, then settled in front of the TV. She no longer watched cartoons, like she did as a kid, but sipped coffee and enjoyed her favorite programs on the Food Network. The celebrity cooks were making comfort food on *The Kitchen*. They made a macaroni and cheese that looked delicious. She and Brody hadn't put that on their list.

She went downstairs at twelve thirty and was happy to see that Luther was eating lunch with them. Paula had made sandwiches and then taken the kids into town to eat. Fast food was a rare treat in their family. Aiden had wrinkled his nose and said, "My mom cooks all the time."

"Someday, you'll appreciate that," Harmony told him.

Ian motioned toward his helper. "You've met our handyman, Luther. Kayla doesn't work on Saturdays during the winter," he explained. "No gardens or yard work to worry about, so she watches the baby, and Luther and I get things done. When she helps Tessa bake for teas when the lodge is open, Luther watches the baby. We keep our hours flexible."

Harmony nodded. "You guys must be pretty easy to work for. You're nice people."

Luther agreed. Eyes slanted away from her, he said, "They treat us like family." He was too shy to look at her directly. She found that endearing.

"I'm flexible, too," Brody said. "When are you starting supper for Tessa? I can stop what I'm doing and help out whenever you need me."

"I'm throwing the pork loin in the slow cooker as soon as we finish lunch." Then she could forget about it and concentrate on her writing.

"Good, what do I get to do?" He sounded excited.

Ian laughed at him. "Probably the same thing Tessa gives me—peel and chop vegetables."

Harmony shrugged. "What can I say? Sous chefs get prep work." When Brody looked disappointed, she added, "I'm using two slow cookers today, though. One for the pork loin, the other for the chuck roast to put in the beef and noodle soup on Sunday."

"Can I work on the chuck roast?" At the moment, Brody reminded her of Aiden.

She gave him a quizzical look. "Didn't your mom let you help in the kitchen?"

He shook his head. "That was her domain. She ruled it with a wooden spoon and was happy to use it as a weapon if we pestered her too much."

Harmony frowned at Ian. "But your mom let you lick the spoon when she made cakes and cookies, right? Tessa said you like helping her bake."

"That was a sacred and special experience," Ian explained. "A rare privilege."

"But you know how to cook."

Ian grinned. "I can grill. And I was single for a long time. I learned a few basics, whereas Brody here married the woman of his nightmares and took her out to dine every night."

Brody scowled and glanced at poor Luther, who was gazing at him in horror. "I *did* marry the wrong woman, and Ian's right. I never learned to cook."

Harmony sighed. "You're making something simple into something difficult. I don't do gourmet. My stuff's everyday food. There's not much to it. You'll see."

They finished their sandwiches, and Ian and Luther took off to work on the suites. Harmony went to the wall of kitchen cupboards and scrounged until she found the stored, electrical appliances. Turning to Brody, she said, "Do as I do." When she set up her slow cooker, he set up his. When she sprayed the bottom and added her roast, he added his. They liberally seasoned the meat with salt and pepper, then chopped onions, carrots, and celery and tossed them in the pot. Finally, she added some chicken broth to hers, and he added beef broth to his. She grinned at him. "I'm going to add a few more seasonings to mine, but all you have to do is put a lid on yours."

"That's all there is to it?" He looked proud of himself.

"For now. By dinnertime, the meat will fall apart. We'll stick it in the refrigerator and shred it for the beef and noodles tomorrow."

Brody cleaned up while she sprinkled a packet of dried French onion soup mix over the pork and vegetables and added a few dashes of soy sauce. "Nothing fancy," she told him. "This is as simple as it gets."

He headed back to work with Ian and Luther, and she zipped upstairs to write. Luxar and Serifina had a bad afternoon. Demons didn't have to wait until the sun set to walk outside. Neither did wizards. Torrid sent both to break down Luxar's door and kill them. Antique wall hangings went up in smoke. So did Oriental rugs and window treatments. Even a few pieces of heavy wooden furniture, but luckily massive stones wouldn't burn, so Luxar's mansion survived. The demon and wizard didn't. Serifina decided there and then that she was going to cast wards to keep enemies from entering Luxar's home. But spell casting took time, and they were barely finished before Harmony had to get ready to go to Tessa's.

She tugged on dark jeans and a crimson, long-sleeved T-shirt with VAMPIRES SUCK in black letters across her breasts. She added mascara and blush, then hurried downstairs. She tossed together a salad and was carrying it from the kitchen when Brody tramped into the foyer and stomped snow off his boots.

"I didn't see you come down." He stopped to read her T-shirt and shook his head. "Is that a good thing or a bad thing?"

She smiled. "Depends on the vampire."

"I have the food loaded in the SUV. You ready?"

She shrugged into her wool coat, pulled on gloves and a hat, then stepped into her boots. "How cold is it?"

"You could freeze your ass off."

She put a hand behind her. "Mine's not that great as it is. I need to protect it."

"I'll stand guard." He took her elbow and hurried her outside. This time, he held the door and let her get settled before he crossed to his side of the vehicle.

"Thanks for the special treatment, but it's too cold for that," she complained. "You can hold my door once spring comes."

"You're holding the salad." He drove carefully to Tessa's.

When they put the roast and vegetables in the center of the table, and everyone took their usual seats, Harmony was happy to see that Tessa looked more rested than before.

Tessa smiled. "I took a nap when I got home from the bakery. I just got up half an hour ago."

"That's good," Ian told her. "Get all the rest you can. Which reminds me. We're sleeping in tomorrow. And even brothers get Sundays off. No working on the suites, and no reason for you guys to bring supper." He looked at Brody and Harmony. "We can all have a break. We have plenty of stuff to reheat."

Brody glanced at Harmony. "Will my roast be okay?"

His roast. Harmony got a kick out of that. "We'll use it on Monday. No problem."

He looked out the kitchen windows at the layers of snow that led to the frozen lake. "How are the main roads? Have you heard?"

Ian grimaced. "We're not total hicks, you know. The country roads might be messy, but the state *does* plow the main roads. I heard they're in good shape."

Brody nodded toward Harmony. "Could we make it to Indy? I didn't make it there the last time I visited. Want to check it out?"

She frowned. "I don't write on Sundays. My brain needs time off. But the weather's . . ."

Brody interrupted her. "It's just as bad in New York, maybe worse. You heard Ian. With my SUV, we'll be fine."

She shrugged. At home, she went out on Sundays, met friends for brunch, spent an afternoon in a bookshop, and usually hit a bar to get a bite to eat. "Why not? I don't have anything planned."

"Good, what if we leave at eleven thirty? It takes an hour and a half to reach Indy, so we can eat lunch there and then look around."

Tessa pushed her empty plate away. "I'm glad you guys are going to do something fun. All you've done so far is work. I want you to like it here, so you want to come back."

Harmony protested. "I'd come back just to see you."

"That's sweet, but I want you to have a good time." Tessa glanced around the table. Everyone was finished eating. "Thanks for supper. It was delicious."

Brody beamed. "We did all right, didn't we?"

"It was perfect. Want some dessert? I brought home cookies from the bakery."

It was Ian's turn to grin. "I love cookies. Can we eat them while we watch a movie? You wanted to rent one online tonight, didn't you?"

Tessa nodded, and they ended up in the living room, watching *The Grand Budapest Hotel*. Harmony loved every minute of it. By the time the movie was over, though, Tessa was almost asleep.

Brody tousled her copper hair. "Go to bed. Take it easy tomorrow, and we'll see you on Monday."

"But I never get to stay up late and really visit with you guys," Tessa complained.

"They should count their blessings. You barf every morning and snore every night." Ian threw an arm around his wife and led her to the stairs. "But we all love you anyway. Have fun in Indy tomorrow, you two!"

They let themselves out. On the drive back to the lodge, Harmony shook her head. "I never realized growing a baby sapped your energy so much."

"Growing a baby." Brody turned the phrase over. "You have a unique way of looking at things."

She gave him a wicked grin. "Do you think your ex is totally wiped out? Isn't that sort of fun, thinking of her as half-dead, dragging herself from one event to another? And in a few months, she'll be huge."

Brody stared at her. "You're evil."

"I know. I write paranormal. Vampires and witches can be ruthless."

He glanced both ways when they passed an intersection. She looked, too.

They had the right of way, but why take a chance? In a few more feet, he began to slow for their turn. "You talk a good story," he told her. "And you have a wicked sense of humor, but scratch the surface, and you're pretty nice."

She shrugged. "Maybe, but my trash talk makes you wonder, doesn't it?"

He pulled close to the front door. "You don't fool anyone for long. Even Aiden's got your number."

She raised her middle finger for him on her way to the lodge. His laugh followed her inside.

Chapter 14

They left at eleven thirty on Sunday. Brody wore his good jeans and a black V-neck sweater. He looked good in black with his ebony hair and smoky-gray eyes. Harmony wore her good jeans, too, and a black blouse. It looked like they'd called each other on the phone to coordinate their outfits. She smiled at that thought.

He glanced sideways at her as he turned for the highway. "What's so funny?"

"We dressed alike. We look like a couple."

He frowned. "Is that so bad?"

"Only for you." Her grin widened. "Girls won't throw themselves at your feet now. They'll think you're with me."

"I am with you. At least for the day." He sounded offended.

"Well, if some girl gives you the eye and you're interested, just tell me to wander around for half an hour so you can get her number."

"I'd never do that. That's rude."

She sighed. "Rude or not, you're single and looking. You have to put yourself out there."

"No."

She stared at him. "Brody, you're a great catch, but girls need to know you're available. Okay, maybe you don't have to worry about that. Girls probably come on to *you*, but why limit yourself?"

He turned onto the highway and blended into traffic. "I want to relax today, to have fun. I don't want to market myself."

She thought about that. "Okay, I get it. If you're doing the come-hither thing, you have to be *on* for it. It takes energy."

"Do you do the come-hither thing?"

"Only at the end of a book, but my days are numbered. Most guys want younger women. Once I creep too much past thirty, I'll have to settle for ice cream."

He laughed. "I don't think so."

"You haven't watched guys in bars. They'd rather go home with a bimbo who can't speak in full sentences than settle for someone who has one gray hair."

"What if the guy's older?" he asked.

"Then they want a girl who wears a Catholic school uniform. They want to feel young again so badly, they stock their shirt pockets with lollipops to get dates."

"You're terrible."

"You already know that. No news flash there." She settled back to enjoy the scenery, but there wasn't much to look at. Finally, she sighed. "Highways can be pretty boring. This countryside's almost flat, mostly snow covered fields."

"If you could travel anywhere, where would you go?"

"In the U.S. or abroad?"

He grinned. "Let's start small. In the U.S."

"I'd drive up and down the East Coast and stop to explore any place that took my fancy."

"Why the East Coast?"

She pursed her lips, considering. "Because I've never done it. I've seen a lot of the West Coast at conferences. And I've been to New Orleans and different places in Florida. I think the East Coast is beautiful."

"I've always wanted to leave New York and drive cross-country all the way to Oregon."

She stared. "How long would that take?"

"If I could, I'd give it a month to wander here and there."

She shook her head. "You need one of those little travel trailers, you know, like the one Lucille Ball used in one of her movies—a home on wheels. Then you wouldn't have to do the great hotel/motel search every night."

"She had one disaster after another, didn't she?"

"Well, yeah, but that was to make it funny."

Traffic started to pick up. He glanced at a road sign. "We're getting close. Ian told me to try the Broad Ripple area. He said it has lots of good restaurants and shops."

Harmony relaxed again and watched different suburbs fly by

while Brody concentrated on his driving. The trip had gone faster than she'd expected. Of course, they'd yakked most of the way. When he finally pulled into a parking spot in Broad Ripple, they decided to check out a nearby restaurant. Leaving the warmth of the SUV, they shivered. The cold bit their skin, but there was no wind. When they pushed through the doors of the eatery, voices and the clink of cutlery greeted them. The air held the warmth of numerous bodies and the aromas of good food.

They didn't have a long wait, and when a hostess seated them at a booth, Brody reached for a menu. "I'm hungry."

"So am I." Harmony fixed him with a stare. "Just so you know, we're going Dutch. I appreciate getting to tag along today, but you aren't paying for me."

His gray eyes danced. "Why? If I pay for your food, will you feel obligated to sleep with me?"

"In your dreams." She grinned. "No, but you buy all the food for the meals at home. I like to pay my own way. I don't like to owe anyone anything. I'm glad I get to cook for Tessa. That way, I get to contribute."

"You have issues. You know that, don't you? You're great at giving, but you haven't learned how to take."

She frowned. "What's so great about taking?"

"Sometimes, it's nice to let the *other* person do the giving. Tessa wanted you to come."

Harmony shrugged. "I know that, and I was fine with staying at the lodge and having supper with her."

"So I'm the one who changed that." His gaze bored into hers. "You don't want to take from *me*?"

She squirmed. "I only just met you. It's different."

He concentrated on his menu. His abrupt silence made her uncomfortable. She scanned her menu, too, trying to distract herself. When the waitress came, Brody said, "We'll need separate checks. The lady's insistence."

The waitress blinked at her. "Okay, why don't you order first?"

Harmony sent an arch look to Brody, but said, "I'll have the seafood Newburg and a glass of Riesling." When Brody stared at her, she said, "I drink whatever I want. I'm no wine expert."

When it was his turn, Brody ordered prime rib and a red wine. The waitress gave them a crooked smile before she left.

Before they could verbally fence any more, Brody leaned forward and said, "Working with Ian on his lodge has made me want a house again."

The abrupt change of subject knocked her off balance. "A house?" Where had that come from? "Isn't that a lot of upkeep?"

He grimaced. "That's the thing. I had a house with Cecily, a monster of a place, but we hired everything done. She loved to entertain, so we had a gourmet kitchen, a cavernous dining room, and a big back patio. I'm not sure I want that again."

The waitress brought them bread, and Brody sliced it and offered Harmony a piece. She spread it with butter, then gave him a troubled stare. "Aren't you putting the cart before the horse? Shouldn't you find a wife and *then* look for a house? Won't she want a vote?"

"How big is your apartment?" he asked.

Harmony snickered. "My place wouldn't tempt anyone. It's under a thousand square feet."

"Do you like it?"

"Well, sure I do, but it's just for me. One person."

He ran a hand through his dark hair. "I'm starting to think I'd be happier with less."

"Yeah, well, you might want to try it on for size before you jump in. You're used to more, to bigger and better."

Their salads came, and Brody stabbed at his lettuce. "What would your dream house look like?"

She shrugged. "I don't have one. Houses entail lawn mowers and fixing roofs and furnaces. Not my idea of heaven."

"If you had a husband? If he took care of things?"

"But I don't. And I won't. So it doesn't matter."

He sighed. "You're no help."

"You're getting downright pathetic, Bro." She shook her head. "Look at you. You're a hunk. You're rich and a decent human being. And you're crying in your salad because you don't have a girl and a house. Go get them."

"It's not always that easy."

"Why not?"

He faltered. "Because sometimes, we want things we can't have."

She looked up, interested. "Ahh, now I get it. You *do* want a girl, but she's not interested in you."

"Maybe."

"Then move on. There are lots of fish in the sea."

He made a disgusted noise. "If I have to, I have to, but I haven't given up yet."

"Tick-tock, tick-tock."

"What the hell is that supposed to mean?"

"It's your biological clock telling you to hustle. I can see it now. You, bent over, trying to chase a football with a toddler . . ."

"Not funny." He reached for his wine glass.

She snorted. "You've wallowed enough for one day. You brought me to Indy to have fun, so start being entertaining."

"Should I perform tricks?"

"Do you know any?"

He let out a long sigh. "You're a difficult woman."

"Tell me something I don't know."

He laughed. "Okay, small talk. Have you read any good books lately?"

They bantered books, movies, friends, and ideas until their checks arrived. Then they walked around the area and ducked into a few shops. Brody found a watch he loved and bought it. Harmony saw a bracelet she liked, but it was forty-five dollars, and she put it back.

"I thought you liked it," Brody prodded.

"I do, but I won't wear it that much. I never dress up anymore."

"Why not?"

She tried to explain. "My friends and I go to small places and bars. We're jeans-type people. We just hang out."

Brody looked around the shop at the variety of jewelry. "But you're not buying anything."

"I don't need anything."

He frowned, confused. "But don't you ever just shop for the fun of it?"

"Not much. I'm sort of over that. It's just more clutter."

A few shops later, Brody saw a tie he liked, reached for it, and then decided against it.

Harmony tilted her head. "I like the colors on that. It would look good on you."

"I have lots of ties."

"That's a nice one."

So he bought it. When they got chilly, going from one shop to the next, they stopped at a coffee shop. They each ordered a dessert, and

Brody paid the bill. He grinned at her. "I'm keeping tabs." Then they decided they'd better head back to the resort.

On the return drive, Brody turned on the radio. They listened to music and the hour and a half flew by. When he pulled to the front door of the lodge, Harmony turned to smile at him. "This was a great day."

"Are you still up for Harry Potter?"

"I don't know. Does it involve popcorn?"

"And wine. I'll sweeten the deal."

"Can I change into my PJs and meet you in the library? We can be comfortable."

His expression shifted. She couldn't read it. Had she offended him? She hung out with guy pals at home and it was no big deal. But his voice sounded relieved. "I love that idea."

"Good, see you in ten." And she disappeared inside. She thought about Brody as she climbed the stairs to her room. The man needed a woman. Maybe if he hung out with her enough, he'd drop some of his reservations and take the plunge. A sharp pang surprised her. What the crap? Close to the heart and deep in the gut. She knew it for what it was. Jealousy. Some lucky woman would snag that man, and he'd be faithful to her for the rest of his days.

When she changed into her oversized button-down top and bottom, pulled on her ratty robe, and stared in the mirror, she grimaced at herself. Brody was temptation on two legs. If she was the marrying type, she'd jump his bones and lick him all over, but she wasn't. So she sure as hell wished him the best. She'd never met a man she liked more.

Chapter 15

When she met Brody in the kitchen, she gulped as a wave of lust hit her. He wore loose-fitting, drawstring pajama bottoms and an oversized, navy-blue T-shirt. His robe was open. How could a man who teased the imagination when he wore jeans look even more appealing in comfy clothes? His black hair was mussed and dark stubble threatened his jawline.

Harmony had spent a lot of time with guy pals. Some crashed at her apartment when they'd had a bit too much to drink. And they'd *never* made her neurons pulse like Brody could. She struggled to keep her hands off the man's bod.

He turned to her when she came up behind him. A smile lifted his lips. "I went decadent and added extra butter to our popcorn."

He could go decadent any time he wanted. She licked her lips. Down, girl, down. *Stop that!* her mind screamed. She went to the refrigerator and got their drinks. "Ready?"

He followed her into the study and put his tray on the coffee table. She handed him his beer, and he started the movie. They both sat in the middle of the sofa to reach their snacks with more ease, and when they leaned back, their shoulders touched.

A pulse throbbed in Brody's jaw. Hmm, interesting. He stretched his legs, and his thigh rested against hers. Harmony tried to concentrate on the movie. *Ignore your baser impulses*, she told herself.

The Goblet of Fire kicked into gear, and it immediately caught her attention. How did Harry Potter's name get pulled from the goblet? How did it get put in, in the first place? The contest wasn't just about winning. It was about surviving the horrible challenges.

Brody took a deep breath and rested his arms on the back of the sofa.

Wait a minute. That's what guys used to do when they took her to drive-in movies. Was Brody making a move on her? She glanced at his profile, but he was focused on the TV screen. He'd driven to Indy and back. He probably just needed to stretch his muscles.

Somewhere later in the movie, when Harry had to face the dragon challenge, Brody's arm slipped and settled around her shoulders. She glanced at him again. Once more, his entire concentration was on the TV screen. Okay, he wasn't hitting on her. He was just totally into the movie. She relaxed and pressed her body against his side. He didn't seem to notice, just turned a little to get more comfortable.

They sat, cuddled together, while Harry went to the baths to learn a clue about how to face the next challenge. Brody chuckled when Moaning Myrtle popped in to help poor Harry, the noise rumbling in Brody's chest. Harmony fought the urge to press her head to his heart or, worse, to climb onto his lap. She was feeling pretty toasty—the room must be too warm—when his cell phone rang.

He reached for it and frowned. Harmony caught the name Carolyn on the I.D. She paused the movie and scooted away to give him some distance.

"Yes?" His voice was cautious, careful. He listened, and his expression turned serious. He glanced at Harmony. He looked contrite. She got the idea. This phone call was personal, and it would take a while.

She waved away his concern. She pushed to her feet and whispered, "We can finish this tomorrow." She handed him the remote and started for the door.

He didn't look happy, but he had something messy to deal with, by the looks and sound of it. She took her wine glass to the kitchen, rinsed it, and put it in the dishwasher.

When she paused outside the study, Brody was deep in conversation. Maybe a good thing. She'd been saved by the cell phone. If she'd sat scrunched against Brody's luscious body much longer, when the movie ended, she might not have been responsible for her actions.

A horrible thought struck her on the way up the stairs. Brody had told her that he was interested in someone, but she didn't return his feelings. What if that someone was Carolyn? And what if she missed him now that he was in Mill Pond?

Fool! Harmony wanted to kick herself. What had she been think-ing? Brody thought about her like she thought about her guy pals. *Get a grip!* But she definitely had the hots for Broody Brody. She shrugged. So what? A romp between the sheets didn't mean any-thing, and if she got lucky enough to give it a try, she'd get it out of her system. So would he, and then he could go back to trying to win the girl who didn't want him.

Chapter 16

Harmony woke early on Monday morning thinking about Brody. Sitting shoulder to shoulder with him last night in their PJs wasn't her brightest move.

She pushed out of bed and padded to her laptop. This was the perfect day for her to be all hot and bothered. Luxar and Serifina were getting it on today. Maybe that's why her mind was so locked into lust. She did a quick rewrite of the scene she'd finished on Friday. A big battle ended with Luxar and Serifina, splattered with blood. When they went back to Luxar's, Serifina headed to her room to shower. Steam was rolling from the hot water when she felt someone step into the shower behind her. Strong hands reached for her washcloth to scrub her back. Soon, arms circled her body and then hands cupped her breasts. She pressed herself against the hard length of her favorite vampire.

Harmony stopped for breath. She strove for new, fresh words to describe the joys of Luxar. Inspired, her fingers flew over the keys. Serifina turned to face him and glued herself to his wet body. Her breasts smashed against his strong chest. Her hips ground against his muscled thighs. Harmony felt her own body tense, tingling with the sensations lucky Serifina was feeling. Luxar's hands roamed, touching everywhere, everything. He bent his head to kiss the base of her neck, to nibble her shoulders. *Slow down*, Harmony told them, but they didn't listen. Supernaturals were so damned horny all the time. *Hey, use some caution*, she warned, but they ignored her.

They barely toweled off before they tumbled on the bed. When they finished the deed, they were as surprised as she was. Serifina was panting, and so was she . . .

And then someone knocked on the door.

Harmony frowned. That wasn't in her plot points. But the next round of knocks came louder, and she realized they were real knocks on the door to her room. *Not now!* "It's open," she called.

Fumbling followed, and then a small kick, and the door opened. Brody balanced a tray that held a plate piled with buttered toast and a few small jars of jam.

He looked at her at the desk and apologized. "I disrupted your work. Sorry. I thought you must be out of coffee cake by now, so I brought you something, in case you're hungry. We didn't eat a real dinner last night."

She took a deep breath. Luxar and Brody had become one in her story. Tall. Dark. Brooding and sexy.

He put down the tray and stared at her. "You look ... disheveled."

She licked her lips. She was hungry, all right. *Come a little closer,* her mind called to him. "I just finished writing a sex scene." That was warning enough.

"Should I be afraid?"

"I'll be gentle, and I respect the word no."

"What am I saying no to?"

She gulped a breath. "I'm so horny right now, I could hump a doorknob. You haven't had any in a while, either. This would be no strings attached. I'll respect you tomorrow morning."

His eyes narrowed. "This isn't payback for buying you coffee and dessert yesterday?"

She snorted. "For that, you'd only get to feel me up."

He grinned. "No regrets or recriminations?"

"Only if you're a dud."

"I'll try to meet your expectations. I don't have a condom."

"I do. They're in my purse."

"In that case ..." He closed the door, crossed the room to her, and carried her to the unmade bed. "Do you always carry protection with you?"

"I'm a writer, damn it. I have to do research."

"Then let's make it thorough." Before she knew it, he'd pushed up her sweater, unhooked her bra, and had his mouth on her right breast. His left hand teased her left nipple. She writhed with pleasure.

"You've done this before," she panted.

"I like to be the best at whatever I do." He gently tugged her sweater over her head, unzipped her jeans, and within seconds, had her naked.

"Tit for tat." She watched as he shed his jeans and shirt. The boxers went next. "Oh, lord."

Another grin. "Now let's see how things fit."

His lips started at her neck, then slid to her shoulder, then to her breasts. His hands explored, stroked, and fondled. He took his time, and she squirmed as each nerve sizzled to life. She felt so turned on, she thought she might blow a circuit. Then he lowered his head to the inside of her thighs, and heat surged inside her. His fingers moved from her nipples and trailed down her stomach. They slid between her legs and her body tensed. He knew just where to touch, to stroke. Her back arched, and he pushed her knees wide. He slid on the condom and was inside her. Her hips rose to meet his thrusts. They pumped until heat exploded inside her. They peaked together, and he sagged onto his elbows. Then he rolled off her and pulled her to spoon against his long frame. Her head fit under his chin, and her feet curled on top of his. She felt cocooned in his warmth, his protection.

He kissed the back of her head. His heavy arm reached over her to hold her close. They lay like that for a while, enjoying the touch and feel of each other. Then he sighed. "Ian's going to wonder what happened to me. If we don't want gossip, I'd better get back downstairs." He moved away from her and stood. He went into the bathroom and took a quick shower, then came to pull on his clothes. She'd risen, too, and slipped on her robe.

Before he left, he turned to her, his eyes glittering with amusement. "The next time you write a sex scene, let me know, and I'll be back."

"Who's Carolyn?"

He tilted his head, studying her. "One of Cecily's friends."

"The girl you're interested in?"

"Hell, no."

"Good." Why did she say that? What did it matter to her?

He rested his hand on the doorknob. "How soon before you finish the novel? You celebrate that, too, don't you?"

Hmm, food for thought. "I'm getting there."

"Give me fair warning and I'll eat a chocolate bar to build up my strength." He nodded toward the toast. "It's cold now, but you'd better eat something to keep up your stamina." And then he was gone.

She stood there, staring at the door. She was used to finishing a book, finding a guy, and having a quickie to celebrate. But this hadn't felt like a quickie. And for the first time in a long time, she wanted more. More sex. And more Brody.

Chapter 17

When Harmony zipped down for lunch, she worried she'd feel awkward, but Paula was in a talkative mood. "Aiden's back to being his happy self about school. Miss Fredericks handled it so well. He thinks the world of her."

Ian shook his head. "I've never met a bully that gave up with just one lecture."

Paula's lips narrowed as she reached for an egg salad sandwich. "The boy stopped hitting and kicking Aiden."

"For now." Ian glanced at Brody. "What do you think?"

"He's laying low so that Miss Fredericks thinks everything's okay."

Paula sighed. "So what else should I do?"

Ian's answer was quick. "Teach Aiden how to punch the kid hard enough to give him a black eye."

"The boy's a lot bigger than Aiden." Paula laid her sandwich on her plate, too upset to eat.

Harmony was starving. She was happy to let them talk while she munched.

Brody turned to her. "What would you do, Harm?"

"Me? If someone picked on me?"

He grimaced. "No one would be stupid enough to do that. You'd think of some creative way to make their lives miserable."

She shook her head. "That's not always a deterrent. My brother was a mean bastard. I learned to stay out of his way."

Brody's expression darkened to a scary mask. "He picked on girls?"

"Only me, he hated it when Mom and Dad made him stay home to babysit."

"And what's he like now? Has he changed?"

"Beats me. We never see each other, but I can tell you this. A kid shouldn't have to deal with a bully. If it was my kid, I might step in."

Brody nodded.

Paula gave them a look. "Just wait till you're a parent. Aiden begged me not to go to his school or to talk to his teacher."

Ian chuckled and nodded knowingly. "Yup, Maeve didn't want Mom anywhere near her school when she got picked on. Calling in your mom is like admitting you're a wuss. It makes matters worse."

"But it's all right to have your big brother step in?" Brody asked.

"Family hangs together." Ian glanced at Harmony. "Well, most of the time. Your brother must have had issues. Maeve's friends knew me. They knew I'd punch any guy who gave her grief and they knew I was crazy enough to enjoy putting mean girls in their place." He paused. "It was pretty fun."

Harmony laughed. Brody would help Maeve out of a sense of duty. Ian thought of it as a way to do something he'd always wanted to.

Paula picked up her sandwich again and mindlessly took a bite. She looked troubled.

Motherhood was a bitch. Harmony shrugged. "You know, we're thinking up things for something that hasn't happened yet. We can brainstorm again if it does. Hopefully, it won't."

Brody and Ian nodded, realizing how much they'd worried Paula. After lunch, Harmony helped carry dirty dishes to the kitchen, then she and Brody started the beef and noodles. At first, their conversation felt stilted. They'd just seen each other naked. Done the deed. But then Brody threw down the forks he was using to shred the chuck roast and blurted, "I just want you to know, you're damn good in bed."

She blinked, caught off guard. "You're nothing to sneeze at either."

"Then there's nothing to worry about." He grinned. "Neither of us are duds. We make a great team."

She stared at him. They *did* work well together, at lots of things. She smiled. "Some guys are weird after they've bedded a girl."

He shrugged. "You laid the ground rules. No strings. No recriminations."

She laughed, relieved. A heavy burden lifted off her shoulders.

He got busy on the chuck roast again. "To teamwork."

She added fresh vegetables and seasonings to the soup pot. He dug through cupboards for the dried, egg noodles and beef broth. When all the ingredients were mixed, she sniffed and gave a satisfied nod, but when she started cleaning up, he frowned.

"What? You don't like egg noodles?" she asked.

"Love 'em, but when do we start the mashed potatoes?"

"You want to put starch on top of starch?" She put her hands on her hips, but couldn't stop the smile that was forming.

He quirked an eyebrow at her and swatted a dishtowel at her ass. She side-stepped it. Serious, he told her, "Soups and stews are cold weather food to help us survive the elements. You can't do them halfway."

"Bull pucky." She shook her head. "The noodles have brought back memories. What did your mom always make with them?"

"When we had beef 'n noodles, we had mashed potatoes and green beans. Always. And she made tapioca for dessert."

"Tapioca? Your mom was thorough."

"You have no idea."

They peeled the potatoes and left them in a pan of cold water to cook later. Brody searched the cupboards, but there was no tapioca, thank the universe for small favors. When they finished up, Brody came to wrap her in a bear hug.

"I've never had a woman friend before. I've been missing out. It's wonderful."

Harmony's heart pounded double-time. A friend. She could do that. No strings. No commitments. Just spending time with Brody. She leaned back to smile up at him, and his gaze was so intense, she stared at him in surprise.

He flicked the end of her nose. "Your guy pals don't know how lucky they are. I've never met a woman who didn't want to change me, who didn't have an agenda for me."

"Change you? Why?" Brody was perfect, as is.

He grinned. "It's what most women do. They always want more."

She shook her head. "People don't change. You get what you get."

"And that's what's special about friendship. It is what it is. No false expectations. I just didn't see it before."

"Is the girl you're interested in a friend?" Harmony blurted.

Brody grinned. "She didn't start out that way, but she is now. A friend with benefits."

Lucky freaking girl. "That's good. If you two click, you'll have a friend for life."

"A friend for life. I like that."

"You think too much, Bro." And Harmony went back to her writing while Brody went to help with suite three.

At five, Brody led the kids into the room for story time. She grinned at him. "You look like the Pied Piper."

"But I'm not stealing them. I return them after you read to them."

Aiden was back to his usual self, stopping to ask questions at every turn. Brody tried to stay as patient as possible, but every once in a while, he'd frown when Aiden stopped the story too close to the time before. They barely made it through the chapter before it was time for them to leave.

"I'll turn on the heat under the potatoes once I drop the kids off," Brody told her.

Harmony wasn't worried he'd forget. The man wanted his mashed potatoes. She didn't bother redoing her makeup and followed him down the stairs. They'd chopped the potatoes in small enough chunks that they only took fifteen minutes to soften. Then she gave him the portable mixer and let him beat them while she added butter and cream. He tasted them to make sure they had enough flavor and smiled his approval. She grabbed two cans of green beans to heat when they got to Tessa's house, and they loaded the SUV and took off.

When they stepped into the house, Ian gave them a small shrug. Tessa came to greet them, and she was crying.

"What's wrong?" Harmony handed the soup pot to Ian and hurried to hug her friend.

"A cardinal flew right into our kitchen window and broke its neck."

"Just now?"

Tessa sniffed and nodded.

"Do you want me to bury it?" Brody asked.

"The ground's frozen, but you could put it in this box and leave it in the garage." Tessa handed him a shoe box.

Without a word, Brody waded through the snow to find the dead bird. Tessa looked out the window to watch him carefully fit the bird into the box and take it to the garage. When he returned to the house, she beamed at him.

Brody removed his gloves and came to hug her. "I love you, sister-in-law."

"Ohhh." The tears started again.

Harmony looked at Ian, alarmed.

"Hormones," he whispered.

Oh, lord! Harmony was great at lending a helping hand, but she sucked at tears and drama. When her parents argued—and they argued a lot—she always took off. She took a deep breath and realized that Brody was watching her closely. She forced a smile. "I hope everyone's hungry. We cooked enough to make scales groan."

Tessa smiled, the tears forgotten. "Let's eat."

For once, Ian encouraged the girls to talk writing. "You've both been pounding away. How are the books coming?"

"Did you see that Sara Addison Allen came out with a new book?" Tessa asked. They both loved her writing and often buddy read her novels when they came out.

Ian looked at Brody and grinned. They let the girls yak away while they dug into the food. When the meal was finished, Harmony stared in surprise at the empty bowl of mashed potatoes.

Brody patted his stomach with a sigh. "I told you that Ian and I love those. It's been a long time since I've had any."

Harmony glanced at Tessa, who did her best to hide a yawn. Tired, again. She tried to give her an out. "Brody and I are watching a movie tonight, so we're going to get going. Thought we'd make it an early night."

Tessa shook her head. "Not this time. Not yet. Give me half an hour. We haven't had a chance for girl talk."

"You look done in." Harmony could watch her friend droop.

"I'm tired of dragging myself around and missing all the fun. Come talk to me."

She grabbed Harmony's hand and pulled her toward the sunroom.

Ian waved them away, went to the fridge for two more beers, and he and Brody went to settle in the living room.

The minute Tessa had Harmony alone, she leaned forward, her eyes gleaming. "Ian thinks you and Brody got it on today. Did you?"

Jeez! Harmony couldn't get away with anything in Mill Pond. "What made Ian think that?"

Tessa's lips quirked up at the corners. "Ian said Brody tried to play it off when he asked why he'd been gone so long. When Ian teased him and asked him what he'd been up to, Brody was so non-committal, Ian knew for sure you two had jumped in the sack. Well? Did you?"

Harmony heaved a sigh of frustration. "We're both of legal age, you know. Neither of us is married."

Tessa clapped her hands. "So you did!"

"It's no big deal." Harmony gave her friend a stern look. "Don't read anything into it. I'd just finished writing a sex scene. Brody walked in right after my characters had a great romp. I was feeling a little . . . needy."

"And Brody said *yes*?"

"I think he was ready for some action, too. A woman called him while we were watching our movie last night." A pang shot through her. Boy, she thought she was past that kind of nonsense. "He's in-terested in someone, you know. He's a little sexually frustrated, too."

"He is?" Tessa bit her bottom lip. "How do you know?"

"He told me. The woman's not interested in him, but he hasn't given up hope."

Tessa grimaced. "Ian didn't say anything about that."

"He might not know. Brody doesn't exactly announce his feel-ings to the world."

"Nuts." Tessa leaned back in her chair, her joy deflated. "I was hoping . . ."

"It's not like that," Harmony said.

Tessa's shoulders sagged. "Bummer."

Harmony grinned. "Not for me. I don't want till death do us part. Getting down and dirty with Brody is the best I've ever had. It's a win/win."

Tessa glared in frustration. "Damn it, Harmony, Brody's a keeper. You should latch onto him and never let him go."

"Like you did Ian when he was with Lily?"

"That's different. They were engaged."

"Don't give me your get-a-man lecture. You sucked at it. You just got lucky."

"Maybe you will, too."

Harmony stood and smiled down at her friend. "Marriage scares the shit out of me. You know that. It's not going to happen."

With a sigh, Tessa rose to walk with her to the door. "Not all men are losers, Harmy. I know the saying that men marry their mothers, women marry their dads, but you're smarter than that. You're smarter than your mom was."

"Quit worrying about me. I'm happy, and I'm happy for you. That's enough." Harmony wrapped her in a quick hug. "And as your friend, I'm telling you that you look like hell. Get some sleep. I'll see you tomorrow."

When they joined the men in the living room, Brody shook his head at Tessa. "You need sleep. Don't overdo. Take it easy. Ian, put your wife to bed."

Ian and Tessa waved their goodbyes as they left, then clicked off the porch light to head upstairs. On the drive back, Brody said, "Ready to finish *Goblet of Fire*? Sorry we had to stop it in the middle."

"I want to see the end, but then I need a Harry Potter break. Can we do something different tomorrow?"

Brody looked smug. "I bought Meg Ryan's movie *French Kiss*. I lost mine at home, and it's one of my favorites."

"I own that movie, too! I love it." Harmony stared at him. "You'd watch a chick flick with me? Even my best guy pals won't do that."

"Really? What do you watch with them?"

"Action movies. Sci-fi. A lot of movies with fast cars and fast women."

He chuckled. She loved that sound, deep and happy. "No History Channel? No war movies?"

"I have my boundaries."

He pulled in front of the lodge and said, "Get comfortable. PJs again tonight?"

If she said no, he'd guess that sitting next to him in flannels had been a turn-on, so she said, "Sure, but if we make a habit of it, I'll have to buy a second pair."

"Not for me. You look cute in whatever you put on."

She could feel heat creep up her neck and stain her cheeks. Damn, when was the last time a guy made her blush? Only Brody. She wagged a finger at him. "That's easy to say before I spill too many things on them."

He reached across her to open the car door. His bicep brushed her breast, and flames shot through her. *Down, girl.* She'd have to sit at the far end of the sofa tonight. No accidental bumping.

He grinned, as if he could read her thoughts. Oh, boy, that wouldn't be good. She gave him her best smile and said, "I'll see you in the kitchen. Popcorn and wine."

His salute was all show. Then she hopped out of the SUV and ran for the door. She'd have to keep some distance between her and Mr. Hunk. He was dangerous for her libido.

Chapter 18

Wind woke her in the early hours of the morning. It screamed past the lodge like a banshee, making the tree branches toss in a mad frenzy. Hail followed, bouncing off the roof and pelting the windows. She got out of bed to stare over the lake. A cracking noise announced a big branch breaking. It fell across the roof of one of the cabins close to the shoreline.

Harmony sank onto the desk chair to watch the storm's fury. When the hail stopped, the snow started. The wind died down, and giant, beautiful snowflakes drifted past the window. She watched until her eyelids grew heavy, and she returned to bed. When she woke at eight-thirty the next morning, the snow was still falling. Mounds of white covered every roof and surface. As she watched, she saw Ian, Luther, and Brody wade through the heavy, wet blanket to reach the cabin. Brody pulled himself onto the porch railing and used the height to hitch himself onto the roof.

Harmony wondered how many push-ups the man did each day. He made lifting himself onto the shingles look easy. Ian stretched to hand him a saw, then followed him up. Okay, Ian had serious muscles, too. Luther tossed a rope to Ian. Brody started sawing on the thick branch, and Ian tossed the rope around it. When the saw blades ripped through the wood, Luther and Ian pulled on the rope to lower the branch to the ground.

The men started on the rest of the tree limb, and Harmony went for another cup of coffee, turned on her laptop, and got to it. There'd be no breakfast delivery today.

By the time noon came, she'd finished a scene, and her stomach was rumbling. How could she possibly want to eat again after the heavy meal she'd had last night? But noodles and potatoes must not stay in your system forever, so she hustled down for lunch a little sooner than usual.

Brody and Ian were already sitting at the small table in the dining room, and Paula was carrying out the tray of sandwiches for them. Grinders. Harmony's mouth watered. The heavens were smiling on her. Then she noticed Brody's expression. Sour. Holy shit, she hadn't seen him that moody since they first met. She turned to Ian.

"Our mom called. Cecily had a miscarriage."

A flurry of questions flew through Harmony's mind. Wasn't the kid lucky he got to go back Home instead of spending years with Cecily and Mr. Money? But Brody was clearly upset. Was he worried about Cecily? Did he still have feelings for her? That thought bothered her. More than it should. More than she expected. Why wasn't he gloating that the woman who wouldn't have his baby lost the baby of a man she married for money? But then, Brody was a good, honorable person. He wouldn't think like that. Did that make her a horrible person because she did? She wouldn't *wish* it on anyone, but Cecily didn't want this baby, not really.

She shook her head. Her time here was getting more and more complicated, making her think about things she usually didn't even consider. She was reading to kids every afternoon, for heaven's sake. But how could she say no to Aiden and Bailey? And she was cooking for her friend. But how could she not help Tessa?

Her heart hurt for Brody. She had no idea what demons he was wrestling, but he was struggling, she could tell. "You okay?"

He gave a curt nod. "Another reminder that life throws us curve balls. Just because you decide you *want* kids doesn't mean it will happen."

Harmony reached to put her hand on his. "It doesn't mean it won't, either."

Ian fidgeted with his napkin. "You can't worry about the negative and let it get to you. You have to hope for the best."

Was he worried about Tessa's morning sickness? About Tessa having a safe pregnancy and a healthy baby? How could a person not worry a little? Harmony patted his hand, too.

Even Paula caught the gloom bug. "There are no guarantees in life, are there? When I met Alex, I never thought I'd marry someone in the military, never thought I'd have his babies and then lose him. It's been tough."

Harmony patted her hand next.

Brody scowled at her. "What about you? Life's offered you your share of bumps. How do you deal with them?"

She swallowed. "Hate to say it, but once I got out of the house I grew up in, I've done everything I can to avoid them."

"I get it now." His gaze narrowed, assessing her. "That's why you stay unattached. If you stay invisible, you'll be safe."

He made it sound like a bad thing. She shrugged. "It works for me."

He ended the conversation by reaching for his sandwich. They ate in silence, and Harmony was relieved when the meal was over. She pushed away from the table and said, "I'm in the middle of writing a scene." A lie, but her laptop was more appealing than their company. "Supper's going to be an easy fix tonight. I thought we'd skip making the chowder and do the enchiladas instead. We need to use the rotisserie chickens. If I cut off reading a little early, they'll be ready in time. Does that work for you?"

Brody and Ian gave distracted nods. She got the hell out of there. As she climbed the stairs to her room, though, she couldn't stop thinking about Brody. He always tried so hard to do the right thing. She hoped life rewarded him for it.

She sat at the desk by the window and read her plot point for the next scene. She'd envisioned the entire thing in her mind. The battles had kept escalating, and Luxar and Serifina realized they needed more help. Serifina's witches and Luxar's allies had been enough so far, but Torrid kept gathering more followers. They needed bigger numbers to defeat him, so when a female vampire who commanded a large brood knocked on Luxar's door and offered to join them, Serifina didn't understand why he hesitated.

Wait. Harmony stared at the words she'd just typed. Luxar didn't hesitate in her notes for the scene. She frowned. What was Luxar thinking? He needs help, and it just arrived. In her notes, he was happy about it. But in her notes, a *male* vampire headed the brood that offered to help them.

Ahh. The ideas clicked in place. Perfect to add more tension to the story. The beautiful vampire had once been Luxar's lover. She left him to start her own brood, but she still had feelings for him. She'd be happy to still be "friends." The chemistry crackled between them, and Serifina sensed it. For the first time, ever, Serifina was jealous, but they needed the help. They couldn't afford to turn his ex-lover away, so they were forced to work together.

As Harmony wrote the scene, she pictured Luxar—with his dark, brooding looks—acting cool and aloof to the female vampire—who somehow looked like Harmony pictured Brody's ex-wife. The scene came out moody and darker in tone. She loved it, but it left her feeling unsettled. When Brody and the kids knocked on her door and burst in, she sent him a sharp glance. Did he still have feelings for Cecily? If she begged him to take her back, promised to have his children, would he? Her glance turned to a glare. Brody blinked in surprise, but settled in his usual chair and lifted Bailey onto his lap.

Reading Harry Potter and interacting with the kids helped her release her pent-up emotions. Damn. How could one scene get to her so much? But then she shot Brody another look. It was his fault. He locked gazes with her, challenging her. Okay, maybe it wasn't. Maybe she was just being irrational. What did she care if he still had feelings for his ex? If he *did* have feelings for his ex, which she was beginning to doubt. Hell, she was beginning to care about him. She wanted him to have a happy-ever-after. That's all. She shrugged her shoulders. Time to get over it and move on.

She finished the chapter and put the bookmark in its place. "I need to get to the kitchen, so we have to cut reading a little short today, okay?"

Aiden gave a happy smile and rolled off the bed. He'd interrupted less than usual today, so Harmony knew the story had grabbed him. "Mom's making tacos tonight," he told her. "My favorite!"

Harmony grinned. Who could compete with tacos? He grabbed Bailey's hand and zipped away, Brody trailing behind them. At the door, Brody turned to give her a quizzical look. "You all right?"

"I'm fine." Her silly jealousy had left her. What the hell was her problem anyway? "I'll be down in a minute."

When he shut the door behind him, she went to the bathroom and squinted at her image in the mirror. Both Serifina *and* the luscious, female vampire would leave her in their dust. She fussed with her hair and makeup a little more than usual, then sighed in disgust and headed to the kitchen.

Brody was leaning against the sink counter, waiting for her. "I didn't know where to start. What do you want me to do?"

Take off all of your clothes and have sex with me on the worktable. No, no, no! She took a deep breath. "What if you shred the chickens and I'll start on the lettuce and tomatoes for toppings?"

"Is that all you want?" His voice was husky.

Damn. Could the man read her mind? Her breath caught for a moment, then she forced a smile. "That's a good place to start."

She showed him how to skin a whole chicken to remove all of the meat. They stood, shoulder to shoulder, as she demonstrated and he worked. He turned to ask her a question just as she turned to watch him, and they stopped, nose to nose, their lips only inches apart. *Kiss me!* she silently screamed. Brody moved closer, but jerked apart when Bailey cried, "Ooh, are you two in love?"

Harmony's cheeks flared bright red, she could tell. They felt like they were on fire. Brody glared at the little girl in the doorway.

"What do you want?"

"Mom forgot the salsa sauce. She sent me to get it." Bailey skipped to the refrigerator and grabbed the jar. She gave them a sassy smile. "Were you going to kiss?"

"Not now. You ruined it." Brody didn't hide his aggravation.

With a giggle, Bailey skipped off.

Harmony started slicing and dicing the fixings to put in plastic containers. Damn, she might as well be under a microscope. There was no privacy here. Brody started shredding chicken with a fury.

In a few minutes, Harmony calmed down. What if Bailey saw them, almost locking lips? It was no biggie. Surely her mom and dad had gotten a little randy once in a while. Harmony added a can of sliced jalapenos to take with them, so others could add them to taste, and the meal wouldn't be too spicy for Tessa. She dug for the sour cream she'd bought and the shredded cheese. After that, she sprayed a roasting pan. She seasoned Brody's chicken and began filling tortillas to place in the pan.

Brody watched, fascinated. Then he joined in. When the bottom of the pan was covered, Harmony opened a large can of mild, green enchilada sauce and covered each rolled tortilla with it. Then she sprinkled them with cheese and turned to slide them in the oven. Brody bent to open its door for her.

She heard footsteps stop at the kitchen door, and Ian's voice. "I'm heading home for the night. You left your watch in suite three, Brody. Here. Catch!"

She caught the movement of Ian's arm as he tossed the watch, underhanded. She shut the oven door and straightened in time to see Brody raise his hand to catch it. His fist stopped inches from her face. He nodded to Ian as he left, then turned to her and stopped abruptly.

"Harmony?" His voice was gentle, tentative. "Are you all right?"

Fear clogged her throat. She couldn't answer. Her heart pounded. Old instincts.

He reached for her, and she planted her feet in a fighter's stance. She pulled her arms up, her hands balled into fists to protect her face. New instincts. No one would ever slap her again.

Brody pushed his arms out at his sides, palms forward, in a defenseless pose. "I won't hurt you. I'd never hurt you."

Harmony took quick breaths, fighting for calm. Brody wasn't her brother. He'd never hit a woman. She buried her face in her hands, and her shoulders shook.

Strong arms wrapped around her. She leaned against Brody's broad chest. He didn't say a word, just hugged her to him. After a while, she moved away from him. She felt stupid. Ridiculous.

"Are you okay?"

Embarrassed, she said, "My brother had a quick backhand. He used it a lot. When he was mad, he used his fists."

Brody nodded. "I get it." He glanced at the clock, purposely trying to break the tension. "Are enchiladas enough? Do we have more food to make?"

Bless him, he was helping her refocus, feel less the fool. She followed his lead. "I like refried beans and a Mexican salad on the side."

"I'll help."

It took a while for her hands to stop shaking. Brody took the knife from her to dice avocados, and she tore the lettuce. With them both working together, they finished just as the buzzer rang for the oven.

Thank God, it was time to pack up and go. Harmony could sit back and listen to Tessa, Ian, and Brody. She needed a distraction, time to unwind.

On the ride over, Brody drummed his fingers on the steering wheel. A little nerve wracking since the roads were terrible. Snowplows had piled white mountains on each side, leaving a narrow corridor in between. They'd added salt and sand, but the winds blew drifts at each intersection.

"I'm sorry I was such an idiot earlier," she said. "I thought the old memories were buried, behind me."

"Life leaves scars." Brody shook his head, back in brooding mode. "We can move past them, but they're there."

"So what's bothering you?" she asked.

He answered without hesitation. "I'm forty. I want kids. I'm not interested in some twenty-something, but if I marry a woman my age, we're taking a risk. If she has a miscarriage, we might have to rule out babies. I thought I had my life mapped out. I'd start a career and make it a success, get married, and have children after we were secure. I never penciled in a divorce. I'm starting to hear the clock ticking, telling me I screwed up."

"So marry someone in their thirties and get frisky on your honeymoon. Make babies."

"I've only met one person who interests me, but it hasn't gone well."

She wondered what type of woman he'd find attractive, but decided not to ask. Today had been shaky enough. She'd finally gotten over the female vampire, and there was no reason to get all steamed up again. Then she laughed at herself for mixing real life with fantasy. Maybe part of being a writer. She *did* feel for Brody, though. One of her close friends had suffered through the same pangs. Gretchen. Of course!

"You know, I have a friend who tried and tried to have babies, but she and her husband couldn't, so they decided to adopt. Now, they have two beautiful kids that they're crazy about."

His fingers drummed faster. "I could love kids who weren't my own, but if I had a choice . . ."

She nodded. "Tessa's brother and his wife don't want kids, and they're perfectly happy. They fill their lives with other things."

"I suppose." He didn't sound convinced. He asked again, "You don't think a time will come when you'll regret you didn't have a baby?"

"If a kid's lucky, my eggs will dry up and die. I have a potty mouth and not all that much patience."

"Kids can live with that. Do you know how many would pay money to have you for a mom?"

"If they're smart, no one."

He gave her a sideways glance. "Well, you're wrong. You don't realize what a great person you are. That's why you push people away, but you don't need to."

What the hell was he talking about? "I don't push people away. I have lots of friends."

"But no one's allowed to get too close."

"That's not because I underrate myself. It's because friends are less stress." On the defensive, she said, "I'm not cut out for family life."

He sighed. "Maybe I'm not either. Maybe that's what the Universe is telling me."

"Bull crap! You're the most wonderful man I've met."

Shit! Shit. Shit. Did she just say that? Out loud? But he needed to hear it and believe it. "I mean, you're going to make some woman super happy." Any woman with a brain and a libido. "You just have to go out there and make it happen."

Brody's fingers quit drumming. He gripped the wheel. "You're right. I need to go after what I want." He gave her a look that sizzled.

Harmony shrank closer to the passenger door. That look felt like an assault. She played back their conversation and fretted. She'd only meant to encourage him. How could that go wrong?

Brody slowed to make the turn into Ian and Tessa's driveway. Ian had cleared it, but its banks were almost as high as the road's. Harmony felt like they were driving through wintry tunnels. She looked forward to seeing Tessa, though. She yearned for small talk and laughter right now. Brody sighed when he cut the car's engine. "Thank God, we're here. I need a distraction. How about you?"

Poor him, she'd infected him with her mood. She needed a glass of wine. Maybe the entire bottle. "My brain feels like a hamster wheel, spinning and spinning. Company sounds great."

His eyebrow rose. "What were you writing today?"

A blush stained her cheeks. She could feel it. "A battle scene." She wasn't above a small lie.

He grinned. "On the field or under the sheets?" Damn, he read her too well. "I can't wait to buy your book."

She'd never considered that. Would he recognize himself as Luxar? She shrugged. "It takes at least a year before a book goes from manuscript to a book shelf. You'll have a long wait."

His smile grew wider. "I'm good at waiting . . . most of the time."

Panic fluttered in her stomach, but then she realized he'd meet someone by then. Somebody beautiful and sophisticated, but warm and funny, too. Someone perfect for him. Her book would be the last thing on his mind. This time, she could return that smug smile. "Whatever, but I don't think paranormal romance is going to do it for you."

He reached across the seat to open her door for her. "This one might."

Yeah, right. In a year, he'd be humping someone to make babies. That thought didn't thrill her. What the hell was wrong with her lately? She'd never been this up and down before.

She got out and lifted one of the cardboard boxes loaded with food. Brody went to get the other one. As they carried them to the house, she bumped her shoulder against him playfully. "In a year, everything's going to look different."

"For both of us."

Ian came out to greet them, but Harmony frowned up at Brody. What did he mean by that? Before she could ask, Tessa stepped out of the house's front door, and Ian reached to take Harmony's load. Then everyone started talking, and the moment was gone.

Chapter 19

The evening sped by before Harmony realized it. Tessa's coloring had improved. "I can keep down food, now that I don't cook it." She patted her still flat stomach. "I'll probably be fat before I know it."

"Not fat." Ian's gaze shifted to his wife's midsection, and he smiled. "You'll look even prettier with a baby bump."

They were so happy *thinking* about a baby, Harmony couldn't imagine what they'd be like once they actually had one. "You two are going to be push-overs for a while. Talk about a spoiled kid."

Ian shook his head in denial. "That feeling goes away really fast when the kid keeps you awake, night after night. Then you switch to survival mode."

Tessa reached for the last molasses cookie. Her appetite had definitely increased lately. "I remember when Darinda had her boys. She was dragging."

Outside the kitchen windows, Brody pointed at giant, white flakes that had begun to fall. "It's snowing again. We'd better drive back before the roads get worse."

He and Harmony didn't talk on the way to the lodge, and she was grateful. She'd wrestled with enough difficult conversations for one day. The evening with Ian and Tessa had been pleasant, and she wanted to hug that feeling to her. He left her off at the door, as always, and after he parked, she watched him carefully cross the lot to the lodge. The pavement was slippery again.

He shook off snow when he entered the foyer. "I know it's January, but the weather isn't usually *this* bad."

"We're going to be lucky if we're not snowbound tomorrow." The flakes were flying harder and faster.

He grinned. "When we were kids, Ian and I always stayed up late, watching trashy, old horror movies when we thought school would be canceled the next day."

"And if it wasn't?" she asked.

"Mom had a hard time getting us up." He smiled, remembering.

"Want to look for some old, trashy movie tonight instead of *French Kiss*?" she asked him.

His gray eyes sparkled. "Are you up for it?"

"No blood and gore, not something like the *Chainsaw Massacres*."

He shrugged. "We'll look for something classy, like one of the *Scream* movies."

She laughed and started to the kitchen. "Popcorn?"

"Pajamas first, you can't watch trashy horror without PJs."

"If we're staying up late, I'm washing my face, too. You'll have to look at me with no makeup."

"That could be scary, but I'll brave it. Meet you back here in a few."

When she came back down, he was already in the kitchen. She could smell popcorn popping, so she wandered in to help him. He'd poured her a glass of wine and had a cold beer on the tray for him. When he noticed her, he stopped to study her.

"You don't need makeup. You're pretty, as is."

"You need to get out more. Anything female is beginning to look good to you."

He laughed. "Come on. We're ready." He heaved up the tray and started to the library. She carried her wine and followed him.

They flipped through channels before they found an old classic—*Seven*—with Brad Pitt and Morgan Freeman. The seven deadly sins, and their punishments, were enough to set a creepy mood. Then Brody found *The Shining*, and you'd have thought he hit the jackpot. "One of my favorites!" he told her. Jack Nicholson doing crazy pushed creepy to its limits. Harmony's eyes were getting heavy when he found *The Mummy* with Brendan Fraser. The movie was scary enough, but Harmony couldn't help it. She fell asleep.

She half woke as he carried her upstairs to her room. He turned down the covers and gently laid her in her bed. She remembered smiling up at him, and then he bent and his lips claimed hers. Damn, the man felt good. She reached her arms around his neck and made the kiss last. But then he pulled away, touched her cheek, and left.

Her dream started with a warm, fuzzy feeling.

She strode through a meadow filled with blooming wild-flowers. A beautiful, white building with columns and green shutters sat on a knoll in the distance, and she walked toward it. When she stepped inside, the bright sunshine disappeared. A forbidding gloom filled its shadowy spaces. There was a mystery she must solve here, she knew. A spiral staircase led to the second floor, and she climbed it, calling to see if anyone was home. On the second floor landing, red smears covered the flowered wallpaper. REDRUM. Chills shivered up and down her spine, but she started down a long, narrow, white tunnel to a room at its end. The temperature dropped the farther she walked.

When she reached the double doors, she pushed on them, and they swung open to a huge nursery. Every cradle held a crying baby. She ran to the first and bent to pick it up to comfort it, and Cecily's face—the way she imagined Brody's ex—stared back at her. She recoiled and went to the next cradle, then the next, and the one after that. Every cradle held an infant that looked like Cecily. This was where Brody's ex and her old, rich husband deposited their many offspring. A baby, wrapped in tapes like a mummy, cried to her, "Only the first son is allowed to live with Mommy." Then every baby jumped out of their cradles, grabbed gleaming butcher knives, and chased her out of the room and down the hallway.

She woke when she tugged on the front door and it wouldn't open. Her eyes did.

She lay in bed, her heart thumping, and vowed never to watch three horror movies, back to back, ever again. She finally left the comfort of her blankets and walked to the window. It had quit snowing. No canceled schools today. She thought of Brody and smiled. He'd have to wake up to his alarm clock. For that matter, she should, too. She was reaching the last fourth of her book. No muse fairies would write her next scene in the morning. The half-moon winked at her. It turned the blanket of snow bone-white. She shook her head. Her vampires were all snug in their fortresses for the moment. No battles tonight.

She returned to bed and slept solidly until her phone alarm woke her. Stretching and rubbing her eyes, she pushed out of bed. This had the potential of being a long day. She was probably going to drag herself through most of it.

She was drinking her third cup of coffee when someone knocked on the door, and Brody poked his head in the room. "Toast and jam?"

She looked at him. He looked tired. "We shouldn't have stayed up quite so late."

He put the plate on the side of the desk and studied her. "For me, it was worth it."

She smiled. "Me, too."

His gaze lingered on her lips. "The kiss was nice."

She felt herself blush, but she nodded.

He bent and grazed her lips again. "Yup, you're definitely worth kissing." He started for the door.

"You're turning into a tease, but we both have work to do."

He paused. "I've never been called a tease before. If you'd like, I could stay and follow through."

Would she! But that wasn't smart. If she had him today, she'd want him tomorrow, and the day after that. "Oh, brother! Have one great tumble with a guy and he wants more. Get out of here. I'm busy."

He chuckled and left, but Harmony's hormones went into overdrive. Her gaze strayed to the unmade bed and thoughts of Brody flooded her mind. She could have him. Right there, in between her sheets. Why hadn't she wrapped her legs around his middle, knocked him flat on the mattress, and had her way with him? Because she was one big chickenshit, that's why. Brody came with an emotional attachment, and she wasn't brave enough to see where that led.

For good reason, she told herself. Emotional attachments made you vulnerable. And she'd promised herself she'd never be vulnerable again. She bit into a piece of toast. *Calm down, girl.* Just thinking about Brody got her all hot and bothered. But Serifina would have a happy-ever-after. She wouldn't. She'd finish her book and go home to her little apartment. And life would go on as always. That's what she wanted. Right? When there was no resounding *yes*, she frowned at her laptop. Someone was going to die today, she could tell. Someone would walk onto the battlefield and wouldn't walk off it. A nice, dramatic death scene would make her feel better.

But that damned, gorgeous, female vampire proved more resilient than Harmony realized. By lunchtime, Harmony still hadn't found a way to kill her off. The character just didn't want to die. Harmony stalked downstairs and plopped on a chair opposite Paula.

Paula stared at her. "The writing's not going well?"

"It's flying off my fingers." Harmony drooled at the stromboli Paula had made. "But the characters aren't doing what I want them to."

Ian shook his head. "Tessa's having trouble controlling her protagonist, too. You were right. There's going to be more sparks in this book."

Harmony gave a knowing nod. "Real life creeps into your stories."

"What's happening with yours?" Paula asked.

Brody leaned forward, all interest. "What *are* your characters up to?"

Harmony tossed him a sour look. "There are more subplots than usual. I think this book is going to have more layers than my other books, but it makes it a little more challenging to write."

Brody shook his head in sympathy. "Too many struggles. Your books always mix romance and battles, right?" He locked gazes with her. "Maybe the heroine should give in to the hot guy so that she can concentrate on defeating the villain."

Smart-ass. What did he know about romance novels? "That's not the way it works," she told him. "The hero and heroine never get together until the end of the book, and then we fade to happy-ever-after."

"But they always get together? No matter what?" His stare was a little too intense.

"For romance, always. That's what readers expect. No, demand."

He relaxed back in his chair. "Then it's worth waiting for the end."

She blinked at him. "In fiction. In real life, things don't always work out."

His gaze held hers. "Then life should imitate fiction."

She looked away. Something had gotten into Brody. He was more assertive than usual today. Maybe he was only mellow when he got enough sleep.

Ian cleared his throat. He looked at Paula. "Were the kids disappointed there wasn't a snow day today?"

His change of subject could never be called *subtle*.

"No, they both love school. I have to admit, I was a little let down, though. I love having a free day with them."

Brody pinched his lips together, serious. "It has to be hard, being a single mom."

"It's not for sissies." Paula nodded toward her apartment in the east wing. "It's a lot easier now that we've moved here. We live where my job is. I know where they are. When we get busy, I hire a girl to keep an eye on them while I work, but they're here, so if something goes wrong, I can deal with it."

"There aren't many eligible men around here, though," Ian said.

Paula snorted. "Doesn't matter. I'm already juggling too many things. I don't have time for one."

"Don't be like me," Brody warned. "Don't wait too long."

Harmony sighed. She didn't need another day of intense give and takes.

Brody reached for a sandwich and shrugged. "Valentine's Day's coming up. Maybe Cupid will take mercy and shoot someone special for us. If not, we'll have to make do."

Ian snickered. "Cupid? Really?"

Brody licked sauce off his lips. "Hey, it makes as much sense as anything else about romance."

They made small talk after that, and by the time Harmony and Brody headed to the kitchen to make shepherd's pie for supper, Harmony was in a better mood. So was Brody. He looked more relaxed again. While she browned the ground chuck, he chopped sweet potatoes to boil.

"Why sweet potatoes?" he asked. "Isn't that different?"

She shrugged. "They're Tessa's favorite. You can use any mashed potatoes to top the meat and vegetables."

When they finished, Ian promised to pop into the kitchen and put the casserole in the oven at the right time, and Harmony went upstairs to wrestle with her story line. In a more benevolent mood, she decided Luxar's ex-lover could live, but it was time to raise the stakes in the battles. Serifina lost one of her friends and fellow witches to Torrid instead. As an added bonus, Serifina was bereft and Luxar showed his tender side to comfort her.

By the time Brody and the kids filed in for story time, Harmony had finished the scene and was feeling pretty happy with herself. She picked up Harry Potter and started reading, looking forward to what Aiden thought about the new chapter, but the boy never interrupted her. When she finished, they still had ten more minutes before the kids had to leave. "Want to start the next chapter?"

Aiden shook his head. "That's okay. I can wait till tomorrow."

Brody frowned at him. "Is everything all right?"

Aiden shrugged and reached for Bailey's hand. His little sister jumped off Brody's lap and gave him a quick hug. Aiden grimaced, but tolerated it. Then they turned to Brody and waited for him to lead them back downstairs.

Harmony brooded. For heaven's sake, she was starting to be like Brody, but something was bothering Aiden, and if he was upset, that bothered her. She shook her head. Hadn't she just read a quote on Twitter, something like "a mother is only as happy as her most unhappy child?" She wished she could remember the source, but it was gone. She understood now how that could be true.

She went downstairs to find Brody. He was looking out the window in the kitchen. He turned when she came in.

"Aiden barely said a dozen words today. If that bully's bothering him again, it's time we take care of it."

She stared. "We?"

Brody dismissed that. "Like you'd sit in front of your laptop if I went to his school without you."

"His school?" She felt like a freaking parrot. Didn't she have any original thoughts? "Shouldn't we talk to Paula first?"

"I already have. It's better if she's not involved."

Now, he had her interest. "What do you have in mind?"

"I'm not sure yet. Ian will have some ideas."

"Ian's ideas will get us all in trouble." She shook her head. "We'll ask him, but I'm not throwing snakes on some kid when he walks down the hallway."

Brody chuckled. "That's been done. We need to be more original."

They took the casserole out of the oven and made a tossed salad to go with it, then braved the slippery roads to drive to Tessa and Ian's. Over dinner, the conversation centered on Aiden and the bully.

Finally, Tessa said, "No one's doing anything until you talk to Aiden. He's a little boy. Maybe a girl with pigtails told him he was ugly today. Or he lost his favorite marble. Who knows? Do your homework first."

Brody reached for the shepherd's pie and dished himself seconds. "We'll talk to him tomorrow."

Harmony nodded.

"We'll be back by story time," Tessa said, "but I'm stealing Harmony and we're driving to town tomorrow. I've been cooped up in this house long enough. I'm feeling better, and I need to get more baking supplies for the shop. I'm getting low on flour and sugar, baking soda. . . ." She waved away her list. "And I want to eat lunch somewhere and maybe shop a little."

"Should you be driving on these roads?" As soon as she said it, Harmony bit her lip. She was beginning to sound like an old worrywart.

Tessa laughed at her. "I'll be careful."

"Take my SUV, not your old pickup," Brody ordered.

"Will do." Tessa rolled her eyes. "I'm pregnant, not disabled. I can still function. And I'm going stir-crazy. I'll pick you up at ten, Harm."

"Harm?" Harmony's voice rose until her friend burst out laughing. For shame. Tessa had lived with Ian too long. "The sitting around has warped you."

The men carried dishes to the sink and rinsed them, and Tessa and Harmony went to the living room to talk plots. They visited longer than usual, and by the time Harmony and Brody left, it was getting late.

"An early night tonight?" Brody asked on the ride home.

"Works for me." Harmony stifled a yawn. It had been a long day. Brody looked tired, too.

He turned on the radio and the station was playing Ed Sheeran's song, "Thinking Out Loud." Brody surprised her by reaching for her hand. "I was listening to that song when I followed you on the country road and you turned into Ian's resort. This should be our theme song."

"You weren't impressed with me when we first met," she reminded him.

"I misjudged blondes."

"We won't know each other when we're seventy." She remembered one of the song's lines.

He gave her hand a squeeze. "Maybe. Maybe not."

She frowned at him, but he sidestepped the issue. "You're going to have fun spending the day with Tessa tomorrow."

She smiled. "I'm looking forward to it."

When they pulled into the resort, he drove her to the front door, as usual. And as usual, she waited for him to join her in the foyer. She wanted to make sure he didn't fall and lie outside, unconscious, on the ice. He stomped the snow off his boots, then walked toward her, pulled her into an embrace, and gave her a long, slow kiss. "I'll still think about you when I'm seventy," he promised.

Her heart felt like it might explode. Her libido wanted to crawl out of her skin. Then he released her and smiled down at her. "Thanks for waiting on me. Get some sleep, and have a great day tomorrow."

On the way up the stairs, she tried to catch her breath. Man, could Brody kiss! She didn't think she was in love, but she sure as hell was in lust.

She had trouble falling asleep that night, and when she did, she dreamt of Luxar and Serifina doing things she wished she could.

Chapter 20

When Brody knocked on Harmony's door in the morning, she was dressed and ready—hair done and makeup on—for her day with Tessa.

He looked her up and down. "You clean up pretty good. I like your sweater."

She smirked. "Do you like the sweater or how snug it is?"

"Both. That color suits you. You should wear blue more often." He crooked his elbow. "I came to escort you downstairs. I have breakfast waiting in the kitchen. You'll want to eat something before a day in the shops."

She blinked, surprised. "That's awfully nice of you."

"In case you haven't noticed, I'm a keeper. I've been house trained, and I play well with others."

"I've noticed. Some girl will swoon." She followed him from the room. "I'm thinking no one takes advantage of you, though."

"Only my ex-wife, and that won't happen again. I won't make the same mistake twice." He glanced down at her. "I take it money doesn't impress you like it did Cecily."

"I never want to be poor, but comfortable's enough. Struggling artists and poverty don't impress me either."

"Good, I can cross them off my list as competition."

She snorted. "You don't need to worry. You're the best of the best."

He frowned down at her, but remained silent. When they reached the kitchen, he opened the oven and took out sausages wrapped in pancakes that he'd kept warm on low heat.

"Holy crap, you went all out!" She sat across from him at the worktable.

"Mom used to make us pigs in a blanket. I love them." He waited for her to dish up, then scooped the rest on his plate. "I'm great at the grill, too."

She shook her head. "I can't grill on my balcony. Against regulations."

"You're missing out in life." He dug into the food.

Harmony slid her last bite of pancake through syrup and glanced at the clock. "Tessa's going to be here in a minute. I'll help you clean up."

"Nope, not allowed. This is your day to have fun. Get out of here, but be back in time to read to the kids, or I'll have to take over, and it won't be pretty."

She laughed. "You'd do fine."

"I haven't read aloud since second grade. You make the story sound good. I'd trip over all the words."

She stood on tiptoe to give him a quick kiss on the cheek. "You're more talented than you think."

"Kiss me more often and I'll practice all kinds of things."

She punched his shoulder. "You *are* a tease. Thanks for the breakfast. See you later." She hurried from the room, and when she reached the lobby, saw Ian pull into the lot to park. He'd driven Tessa so that she could take Brody's SUV today.

Harmony was pulling on her coat when Brody came to dangle the keys in front of Tessa.

"Drive carefully. The roads are bad. I'm not worried about the SUV. It's insured, but it's carrying two of my favorite people."

Tessa wrapped him in a hug. "I love you, too. We'll be back by five, and then you can quit worrying."

He grinned, and Ian went to stand next to his brother. "Have fun, you two!"

With quick waves, the women headed out the door. Once in the vehicle, Tessa grinned. "I have a grocery list, and I have money. Let's get the hell out of here."

Harmony laughed. "Someone's been cooped up too long."

Tessa pointed to different farmhouses on the way to town. "That brick house is the Albertsons' place. They run a dairy herd." The house looked so solid, it could hold off armies. She pointed to a farm on the other side of the highway with two silos. "The Kruses grow corn, soybeans, and wheat. Their granddaughter's in Bailey's class at school." A little farther on, she nodded to a big, square white house with three red outbuildings, large fenced-in pens, and a huge pond. "The DeLanceys raise ducks, geese, quail, and chickens. We buy all four kinds of eggs from them."

"Geese eggs?" Geese must lay eggs, right? But Harmony had never considered eating one for breakfast. "Do they taste different than chicken eggs?"

Tessa smiled. "Not really, but it's fun to boil them for Sunday brunches at the resort and let people ogle them."

When they reached the edge of Mill Pond, Tessa nodded at a corner gas station/garage. "Garth's the best mechanic in town. He's a good friend of ours."

Harmony shook her head. "You know every single person who lives here, don't you?"

"The joys of a small town," Tessa said. "You'll meet a lot of them soon."

Harmony stared. "Why?"

"Chase's bar is open for lunch on Wednesdays, just one day a week, every week. He smokes pork and does barbecue. It's the only thing on the menu. It's always packed. We'll see half the town there. What do you think?"

Harmony could miss half the town, but Tessa was probably ready to catch up with old friends. And there was pulled pork . . . "Works for me."

Tessa grinned. "Don't fix too much food tonight. I'll be stuffed."

"Yeah, right, I've seen you eat. I'd nickname you Miss Piggy, but you're eating for two."

Tessa threw back her head and laughed. "No one picks on me like you do. I love it!"

Before they hit the grocery story, Tessa parked downtown where all the small shops circled the courthouse. "Mind if we look around?"

"I'm just along for the ride. Why not?"

The sidewalks had been cleaned and salted, so they walked from one little shop to the next. When they reached the baby and kids' clothing shop, they both sighed with pleasure.

In an antiques shop, Harmony went straight to a cradle. The bed dangled and rocked from two, sturdy columns. "Is it too soon for me to buy you a baby present? Is that good Karma or pushing your luck?"

Tessa's hazel eyes misted as she pushed the wooden bed. "It's beautiful."

"Can I get it for you?"

"Yes!"

They loaded it in the back of Brody's SUV, then trudged around the rest of the block, stopping to look in each shop's window. By the time they returned to the vehicle, Harmony's toes stung from the cold, her nose could rival Rudolph's, and her cheeks were way past rosy.

Once behind the steering wheel, Tessa hugged herself. "Darn, it's cold. Let's go buy groceries. We'll be inside the whole time."

Harmony nodded. She needed to thaw out. She was almost warm by the time they hurried inside the store. When she'd first come here with Brody, she'd been surprised that it wasn't bigger. A super store sat on the fringe of her town in New York. It took an hour to make it from one end to the other. But she and Brody had found everything they needed here, and that's all that mattered. She wasn't cooking anything fancy enough to need specialty items.

Tessa pulled her list from her purse, and Harmony gaped. Tessa chuckled. "Don't worry. I'm a regular here. I called Art ahead, and he has all my baking stuff, ready to load."

"Art?" Harmony asked.

"The owner/manager. His kids, Mark and Michelle, help out. Mark will load everything while I get the everyday items on my list."

Harmony had never thought about how many pounds of flour and sugar Tessa went through each week, but she baked one hell of a lot of pies, cakes, and cookies. As they wandered down one aisle after another, Harmony said, "What if I make quiche tonight? Is that light enough?"

Tessa nodded. "We'll buy some take-home, smoked meat from Chase for the boys. That'll keep them happy."

By the time they finished and went to check-out, the girl at the register was ready for them. "Dad and Mark have everything in the back of the SUV, and Mark said to call him when you were ready to leave."

Tessa frowned. "Call him? Why?"

Michelle grinned. "Because we heard that you're pregnant, and he doesn't want you to lift anything heavy."

Tessa laughed and shook her head. She turned to Harmony. "There are no secrets in a small town."

A stocky, young man who looked a lot like the older man walking next to him came to greet them. "Congratulations!" the three store people said together.

"Thanks." Tessa tried to convince them that she and Harmony could handle the groceries themselves, but Mark wasn't hearing it. He pulled on his winter coat and insisted on helping them.

When Tessa blew him a kiss and pulled away, she sighed. "Cities might have more to offer, but small towns can be pretty special, too."

Their next stop was Chase's bar, and just as Tessa had predicted, the parking lot was full. When Tessa entered the room, people stood up and clapped. Her blush crept up her neck all the way to her hairline, and Harmony laughed at her.

Chase himself came to get their order. He smiled at Tessa. "You and Ian will make beautiful babies together, but ours would have been better."

She shook her head at him. "Chase, meet my friend, Harmony. Harmony, our local player, Chase Carlton. All the girls love him, and just so he doesn't get any ideas"—she gave a stern look to the good-looking, blonde bartender—"my friend came here to catch up on work, not to have a fling."

His smile was easy, inviting. He'd nailed the surfer look with his laid-back style, sun-streaked hair, and sexy stubble. His blue-green eyes sparkled as he cocked his head at her. "All work, no play? Sounds dull."

"I'm a slave to my writing. What can I say?" Harmony liked him. He'd be a fun time in bed when she finished her book if she didn't have someone else in mind.

He shrugged. "If you change your mind, I'm here. I do my best to keep customers happy."

She laughed. "You're good. I bet you have *lots* of happy customers."

With a grin, he gave her a quick salute, then turned to Tessa. "Should you be eating barbeque? I've heard you had morning sickness."

Tessa rolled her eyes. "No sauce for me, just a pulled pork sandwich."

His gaze returned to Harmony. "Are you delicate, too?"

"Hardly. Give me the works."

He gazed at her suggestively. "Do you want a pickle spear with that?"

Oh, boy. "Make mine a double."

He laughed. "I'll be right back with your order, ladies."

The minute he left, Tessa leaned closer and whispered, "Don't let Chase fool you. There's a lot more to him than meets the eye."

Harmony grinned. "You like him, don't you?"

"A lot. He's a good guy, sort of like you. He's smart and funny, but tries to keep things simple. Doesn't want to get too serious. That's changing, though. I get the vibe he's starting to want more."

"Then he's not for me."

Tessa grimaced. "I want you to be as happy as I am."

"I'm happy enough, and I don't listen to lectures in bars."

Thankfully, people started drifting to their table, a few at a time, and Tessa's attention went to them. There were lots of congratulations and lots of introductions. By the time their food came, Harmony had heard enough small talk and was ready to dig in.

She took a bite and moaned with pleasure. "This guy knows how to cook."

Tessa nodded, too busy eating to talk. The sandwiches were huge, piled high with smoked pork. Homemade chips with a special dip and coleslaw came as sides. No wonder Tessa warned her not to cook much for supper.

They were only halfway through their meals when people started clearing out. Tessa guessed most of them came early. The rush over, Chase came to pull out a chair at their table. "Well? Do you like it?"

Harmony licked her lips and grinned. "Some of the best I've ever had."

He winked. "That's what all the girls say."

She shook her head. "How long have you owned the bar?"

"I grew up in it. My parents bought the place and raised me in it. Our apartment's on the second floor."

Harmony hesitated. She was curious about his parents, but didn't want to bring up what could be a sad topic.

He gave a half smile. "They retired to Florida, live on the beach. They'd made enough burgers and fries, poured enough beers."

"You're only in your mid-thirties, aren't you? Are they old enough to retire?"

"They had me late. I have a feeling my wild ways wouldn't impress them at all. They left me in their dust. Had to get it all out of their systems before they hitched with each other and started their business."

"I'm glad it worked out for them." Harmony liked happy-ever-afters. That's why she wrote romance.

"How long are you staying in Mill Pond?"

"Till the end of the month, I came to finish a book on deadline."

"And no time off for good behavior?"

"I spend that catching up with Tessa. We go back a long time."

His gaze settled on her copper-haired friend. "I'm happy for you, Tess. You found the right guy. And now you're starting a family. Congrats."

Tessa studied him. "What about you? Are you getting ready to settle down?"

He grinned, but his gaze was pensive. "And deprive women of good times and gratification? I'm not that cruel."

Tessa leaned forward and put her hand over his. "You'll find her, Chase. And she'll appreciate you."

He grimaced. "Now you're getting maudlin on me. Time to clear the tables." He gave Harmony another wink. "Remember. I'm here." And he went to the kitchen to grab a cart.

They left money on the table, then set off to head back home. Harmony's thoughts revolved around Chase. A few weeks ago, she'd have thought she'd died and gone to heaven if she met him. He was still tempting, but not enough. And that surprised her.

When they reached the lodge, Ian came outside to greet them. "Leave the groceries in Brody's SUV. He said he'd drive them over tonight, and we'll unload them then. Nothing will spoil. It's too cold." He saw the baby cradle and grinned. "That'll look perfect in our room."

Tessa was losing energy. Ian looked at the dark circles under her eyes, and said, "What the hell? I'm leaving early and taking you home, so you can take a nap. I'll drive Brody's SUV, and he can drive my truck. We'll trade back tonight." He handed Harmony his keys and loaded Tessa back in the SUV. "See you tonight."

Harmony went to tell Brody the news. She found him, working in the third suite. He wore old, ripped jeans. He'd taken off his sweater and a short-sleeved T-shirt was plastered to his hard abs. His biceps bulged as he mudded the dry wall. She licked her lips. Construction sites should provide drool bibs. A girl could dehydrate.

He finished smoothing a wall and glanced her way. He stopped, surprised. "I expected Ian."

She told him about the new plans. With a nod, he said, "Tessa probably overdid it today. She needed some fun."

"Will quiche be okay tonight? Tessa didn't want anything heavy. She brought home some pork barbeque, too."

His lip curled on one side. "Men have been enlightened. Real men *do* eat quiche these days. I'll be fine."

"I'm going to start it now, so it's done before the kids come up," she told him. "I have plenty of time, so if you want to finish in here, we can divide and conquer."

"You won't mind? I'm the one who signed you up for supper duty."

She smiled. "I know, but I'm not going to even try to write today. It's no big deal." She'd made it past a hundred and seventy pages. She'd written in fits and starts, but the words were piling up.

His gaze turned thoughtful. "Thanks. Really. I'd like to finish mudding both suites, then we can sand it tomorrow."

She gave him a wave. "See you for story time."

It felt odd to work, alone, in the kitchen. She did it all the time at home, but this kitchen was so big, so impersonal—a restaurant kitchen. It was too quiet. She turned on some music and that helped.

Once she started crisping the bacon and working on two crusts, she settled into the joy of cooking. Her pie crusts were nothing fancy. Chefs on the Food Network would cringe, but her grandmother had taught her to cut one cup of cold shortening into three cups of flour with a pinch of salt, then add ice water until it formed a ball. She rolled the dough into circles for two pie plates. All she needed were bottom crusts. She pricked them and put them in the oven for ten minutes before she added the filling.

She mixed eggs and milk, cheeses and bacon, and sang along to the radio. Once the quiches were in the oven, she filled the sink with soapy water and started cleanup. She danced to the music while she dried bowls and beaters. She was wiggling her hips and moving her feet when Brody came to help her. A big grin split his face, and he took her in his arms and danced her around the kitchen. For a big man, he was light on his feet.

He took a deep breath. "It smells wonderful in here."

"Bacon does that." When the music broke for advertisements, Harmony laughed. "You dance really well."

He bent her into a dramatic dip. "I've been told I have great moves and lots of rhythm."

When he righted her, she shook her head. "You're a man of many talents. Reading aloud might not be one of them."

He laughed. "See? We complement each other. Your strengths are my weaknesses."

"Either that, or you'd rather not read to kids. I've noticed men don't learn to do things they don't want to." The timer on the oven buzzed, and she went to check her quiches. The filling was set, and the crusts were golden brown. Perfect.

He glanced at the steamed windows over the sink. "You've heated up the place, but then, you always do."

She shook her head and put the quiches on the counter to cool. "It's easy to get you excited. All a girl has to do is dress up a little, but I'm going up to change before the kids come for story time. I'm ready for my baggy jeans." She stopped to check him over. "Speaking of which, I must say, you look awfully good in what you have on."

He flexed his arm to make his bicep bulge. Oh, Mama! If he weren't so full of himself, she'd have reached out to touch it. Muscle, muscle everywhere. But he didn't have a self-esteem problem, so she just nodded. "Nice."

"You love it, I can tell."

She did love it, but she wouldn't tell him that. "You're too much! I'm leaving you. Try to control yourself during story time."

His chuckle made her heart skip. She loved that sound—deep and masculine. She turned and retreated. Brody was too tempting.

Once in her room, she slid into her old jeans—no rips, but worn and forgiving. After the big lunch at Chase's bar, the waistband on her good jeans was too snug. She tugged off her blue sweater and pulled on a stretchy, thermal top. She kicked off her good boots and wiggled her stockinged toes.

When Brody led the kids up at five, he still wore his ripped jeans and T-shirt. "You didn't dress up to go to Tessa's?"

"Not for barbeque. I want to look manly when I eat quiche."

She rolled her eyes, then frowned when Aiden sank onto the side of her bed and didn't stretch out on his stomach to kick his feet in the air. Brody's jaw stiffened. Oh, boy. There was a storm brewing, and Brody meant business.

Chapter 21

Harmony reached for the book, but before she could open it, Brody said, "What's the deal? Did your teacher blow it, Aiden?"

Aiden sat up straight, going into defense mode. Smart move on Brody's part. He knew the boy would stick up for his teacher. "She talked to Dirk. He doesn't hit or kick me anymore."

"Then what does he do?"

Bailey squirmed on Brody's lap, and Aiden gave his little sister a look that said *Shut up!* She stuck out her tongue at him. "He pinches him instead."

Aiden glared.

Bailey reached for his hand. "He hurts you. I don't like him. If I see him in the cafeteria, I'm going to kick him."

She would, too, Harmony was sure.

Aiden scowled at her. "Stay away from Dirk. He's mean."

Like Harmony's brother. He always needed to hurt someone.

Brody had heard enough. "Show me." The man's tone could freeze hell.

Aiden pulled up his T-shirt's sleeves to reveal multiple bruises.

Harmony felt her lips thin. She could think of a myriad of ways to deal with Dirk—making him walk across hot coals, tossing a fireball of magic at him that would leave a *big* bruise—none of them practical. Grabbing him by his shirt collar and shaking the living daylights out of him would probably get her in trouble. How much trouble? No, out of the question.

Brody's tone turned smooth and friendly. She narrowed her eyes at him. "You know, Harmony and I have never seen your school. We're both curious what it looks like. We could watch you play if we got there around morning recess time."

Aiden wasn't fooled. He crossed his arms. "You can't be mean to Miss Fredericks."

Brody looked shocked. "We know how much you like her. We'd never do that."

"You can't beat up a little kid either."

Brody spread his hands in a helpless gesture. "We won't even talk to him."

Aiden bit his bottom lip, trying to decide. "I'll tell you if you teach me how to hit."

"Why do you want to learn that?"

"After Miss Fredericks told Dirk to leave me alone, he kicked Jake. Jake punched him back—hard. Then Dirk started pinching me." He sighed. "I'm smaller than Jake, though."

Brody looked thoughtful. "I can teach you how to punch, but Ian took karate. Size doesn't matter as much with martial arts. Maybe we'll both spend an hour with you, if your mom says it's all right."

Bailey turned on Brody's lap. She looked at his muscles. "Do you punch people?"

"Not anymore, but when I was a boy, I got in a few fights."

Bailey gave a wise, five-year-old nod. "Me and my friends will help Aiden. We'll jump on Dirk."

Aiden closed his eyes, and Brody tousled the little girl's fine, black hair. "Sometimes, a guy has to fight his own battles, or other guys tease him that he can't do it alone."

Bailey pursed her lips, torn. "That's just silly."

"I didn't say it was smart, but that's the way it works." Brody gestured to Harmony, and she started to read. Aiden flopped on his stomach and lifted his legs, swinging them when tension mounted in the story. He didn't interrupt like he usually did, but he looked more relaxed, knowing help might be on the way.

When they finished the chapter early, Brody herded the kids toward the door. "Let's go talk to your mom." He looked at Harmony. "If Paula says it's okay, can you drive to the school with me tomorrow?"

"I wouldn't miss it."

He smiled. "See you at six."

Each kid took one of his hands, and out they went. Harmony went to the window and looked out at the snow-covered yard and frozen lake. She hoped Paula would be all right with Brody and Ian teaching Aiden how to defend himself. And she hoped the idea worked. What if Aiden punched Dirk, and it only made him madder and meaner? Then they'd have to think of something else, because no boy should be hit, kicked, and pinched at school—or anywhere. If she had to buy garter snakes to put in Dirk's desk, she'd do it. She'd pay a big bruiser boy to pound him, if she had to.

She checked her e-mails and Facebook page before she went downstairs at six. She was behind, but not buried. She and Brody bundled up, collected the quiches, and headed to Ian and Tessa's. The wind had created a crust on the snow, and their footsteps crunched on their way to the house.

Brody grabbed Ian's shoulder the minute they stepped inside, and the two brothers bowed their heads together for a serious talk. Tessa gave Harmony a questioning look.

"A bully's picking on Aiden," she explained. They went to the kitchen and put the quiches on the table. Harmony grimaced and handed Tessa a bag of salad greens. "I got lazy and just brought the bag."

Tessa dumped them in a bowl. "As long as I don't have to make anything, I don't care."

The guys joined them, looking smug.

Tessa shook her head. "What are you going to teach Aiden?"

"How to flip someone. That should surprise dirty Dirk." Ian grinned. "And if that's not enough, I'll teach Aiden how to do real kicks."

"Let's hope it doesn't come to that. And Paula's okay with that?" Tessa eyed her husband with suspicion.

Brody sliced the quiche and started dishing up. "Paula's not too into her son being a victim. She's happy with him learning a few moves, said her husband would have taught him, if he was still alive."

When everyone was served, Tessa glanced at Ian, her expression wistful. "Every parent probably wants to shield their kid from any hurt or harm, but it's a tricky balance, isn't it? We can't fight all their battles for them."

"No, but we can help *them* fight them." Ian divided the pulled pork between him and Brody. "Dirk's going down."

Tessa tilted her head, studying him. "For all your laid-back charm, I wouldn't go up against the McGregor brothers."

"Damn straight." Ian pointed his fork at Harmony. "This quiche is really good."

"Thanks." She shifted the talk to their day in town, whom they'd seen, and the latest news.

Ian frowned. "Grams didn't meet you at Chase's? She hasn't been meddling enough lately. What's she up to?"

Tessa glanced at the wall calendar. "She's in charge of the big fund drive for the arts. She twists the arms of business owners to donate products for an online auction. You donated a free weekend at the resort."

"I did?" Ian looked surprised.

Tessa nodded. "And I signed up to ship two dozen cookies to a winner each month for a year."

"Can I sign up for your cookies?" Harmony asked.

Tessa laughed. "Sure, the auction goes online the first Friday of every February. Carl Gruber's donating a dozen, hand cut steaks." She looked at Brody. "Carl raises Angus beef cattle. Evan Meyers does specialty cheeses. Harley sends bottles of wine." She shrugged. "It's an impressive list."

Harmony blinked, impressed. "No wonder I haven't met your Grams. She must be buried every January."

"She likes it. She doesn't like to drive in bad weather, so she can stay home and keep tabs on everyone while she prods them for donations." Tessa shook her head. "And I used to wonder where my mom got the social bug."

Brody grinned at Ian. "Our mom's the same way. Maybe it skips a generation. Neither of us got it."

When dinner was finished, Ian said, "Harmony, come upstairs and see how the cradle you bought Junior looks in our room."

"Junior?" Brody groaned. "You wouldn't."

"I might." As Ian said it, Tessa shook her head, but the brothers kept bickering.

"What if the baby's a girl?"

Ian's brown eyes glittered with humor. "Then we'll call her Juney."

"Ugh." Brody crooked an eyebrow at Harmony. "You bought them a cradle?"

As they climbed the stairs, Tessa explained about finding the perfect one in an antique shop. When Brody stepped into the room and saw it, his expression softened.

"It's beautiful." He rubbed a hand over the smooth wood.

Ian looked at his brother's face and said, "Come on. I need some ideas for the nursery." He led him to a room across the hall.

Tessa stood with her hand resting on her stomach. She turned to Harmony, tears misting her eyes. "I can't believe how much my life has changed, and it happened so fast."

"All for the good?" Harmony couldn't tell if the unshed tears were happy or not. Had the hormone peaks and plummets returned? Or was Tessa more emotional because she'd tired herself out?

Tessa sagged onto the mattress and motioned for Harmony to sit next to her. "I thought I was so smart, protecting my heart, guarding myself from any pain, but I was so wrong. I'd have never known what I missed if Ian hadn't been so . . . him."

Harmony smiled. "It's awesome to see you so happy."

"There's nothing like it, nothing to compare it to." Tessa squeezed Harmony's hand. "I'll quit now. I know how crazy it makes you when people get all mushy."

"You deserve this happiness." Harmony leaned her shoulder against her friend's. "You've earned it."

Tessa gave her a long, hard look. "So have you. More so."

"Nope, don't go there. Don't be one of those people who finds Mr. Right, then tries to convert all of her friends."

Tessa took a deep breath. "Okay, I'll resist, but I'm right."

Harmony waved that comment away, then asked, "How far are you in your book?"

Tessa laughed. "You're trying to distract me with shop talk."

"Did it work?"

"A little over halfway. What about you?"

Harmony frowned. "That's what you told me the last time I asked. Are you getting any writing time?"

"Plenty of it, but I keep falling asleep. It's funny how I don't type when I'm snoring."

Harmony sounded smug. "I've got you beat. I'm one hundred seventy-five pages in."

"Smart ass."

The talk turned to plots and pacing for the next fifteen minutes until Brody stuck his head in the room. "We'd better go. The temperature's supposed to hit bottom tonight. I'd like to be back at the lodge."

"Zero?" Harmony asked.

"Minus two. By the time the SUV heats us up, the drive will be over."

She nodded, and they followed Brody downstairs. Ian pressed a bag in Brody's hand. "Two loaves of nut bread. I don't know what you've been scrounging up for breakfast, but these might help."

When they walked outside, the cold took Harmony's breath away. The air felt dry and sharp. It cut her lungs when she inhaled. Her teeth chattered on the drive home, and she felt sorry for Brody when he parked in the lot and had to make his way to the lodge. He rubbed his ears, red from the cold, when he got inside.

"Wine or tea tonight?" he asked.

"You make tea?" Something hot sounded wonderful.

He hung up his coat and started to the kitchen. "I can pour hot water over a bag. Let's see what's in the cupboards."

She chose wild berry zinger, and he went with Earl Grey. They sat at the kitchen table, cradling the mugs in their hands to warm them. When they finished, Brody went to get a bottle of wine out of the refrigerator. His gaze settled on her thoughtfully. "I figure you for the kind of friend who gives as well as takes."

Uh-oh. Harmony eyed him with suspicion. "I like to think so. Why?"

"Paula and the kids are asleep. You wanted to celebrate when you finished a spicy chapter, and I was happy to oblige. Well, I finished all of the mudding in all of the suites today. Mudding's a bother, so I think I deserve to celebrate, too."

She could feel a smile form. "Do you? What do you have in mind? A back massage?"

"That would work . . . if you're naked . . . and in bed." He grabbed two glasses.

She stretched. "I am tired."

"I don't intend to let you sleep."

She looked him up and down. "You *do* look sexy in your torn jeans." She rinsed their tea mugs and put them in the dishwasher. Then she started for the stairs, swinging her hips more than usual. "I'd never want to be called a fair-weather friend."

He grinned. "I didn't think so. You're more like a friend in need."

The thought of Brody in her bed sent her nerves buzzing. "Fair is fair. You're always there for me." She pushed her door open, and when he stepped into the room, she smashed him against the wall for a fierce kiss. The fun and games were over. She'd thought about this for too long.

He gripped her with his free hand, pulling her closer. They stayed locked together until they both had to come up for air. He fumbled forward, kicking the door shut, and put the wine and glasses on her coffee counter. Then he reached for her again. Witty small talk was forgotten. Passion pulsed in the room. She could hear it.

"You wanted a massage, if I remember right." She tugged off her thermal shirt and jeans. Her bra and panties fell next, then she bent and took off her socks. His clothes flew as he tried to keep up and watch at the same time.

She yanked the comforter lower on the bed. "Stomach down," she told him.

He lay flat, and she positioned herself on her knees, straddling him. Holy Muses, what a gorgeous stretch of male. She could stare and drool for hours, but there were other pleasures that were more active. Bending forward, she began rubbing the corded muscles of his back. She tried to apply pressure, but quickly realized all he cared about was her touch. His muscles trembled every time she stroked them. Well, she could do better than that. She stretched herself on top of him, smashing her breasts against him, and began nibbling his neck. His breath came in short gasps as her hands explored over and under him. Finally, he groaned and rolled, taking her with him, so that he was on top, his weight resting on his elbows. He lowered his head, and his lips roamed from the top of her eyelids to her inner thighs and back again. When he moved to his side, it freed his hands, and then his lips and fingers explored in tandem. She squirmed when his mouth teased the base of her throat while his fingers played with her nipple. Her skin grew hot. Her insides melted. Nerves stretched and hummed. She held her breath. Every cell, every pore, longed for release.

His clever fingers slid between her thighs, massaged and teased, then pushed inside her. She spread her legs, inviting more. When he positioned himself and filled her, she arched her back, timing her thrusts with his. They peaked in unison, and when they finished, he spooned her against him.

They lay there a long time, content, until Brody finally stirred. He opened the wine bottle and poured them each a glass. They sat next to each other, propped against the bed pillows, and sipped in silence. When they finished, she could hardly keep her eyes open. What a beautiful day from start to finish! Shopping with Tessa and sleeping with Brody—it didn't get much better.

When they emptied the bottle, he got up, pulled on his clothes, and bent to kiss the top of her head. "Thanks, that was perfect." And he quietly left.

She sighed. All of a sudden, the bed felt too big, too empty. She rolled onto his pillow and breathed in his scent. Nuzzling under the blankets, a smile curled her lips as she drifted to sleep.

Chapter 22

Harmony gave herself more time than usual to get ready in the morning. She and Brody were driving to Bailey and Aiden's school for Aiden's first recess. She used the diffuser to blow-dry her hair, scrunching it so that it waved. She pulled on her good jeans, a red cashmere sweater, and her dress boots. She wanted to look respectable if they met Aiden's teacher. When she walked down to meet Brody, he gave a low whistle.

She grimaced. "I'm supposed to look like a responsible adult."

"You nailed that . . . and more." He motioned toward the kitchen. "I told Paula and Ian that we wouldn't be here for lunch. I thought we'd grab something in town."

"That'll be fun. Tessa really likes the diner."

"So does Ian. Nothing fancy, I guess, but good food." He crooked his elbow for her. "The car's waiting."

As usual, he had it pulled to the door and heated up. There were perks to having a hot guy drive you to town. The air was cold, but not freezing. "Do you think kids will even have recess today?" she asked.

He held her door and waited for her to settle on the heated seat—sheer heaven—before he went to slide behind the wheel. "Aiden said they had recess yesterday, and it was colder than this."

"Poor kids."

He waited for three cars to pass, then pulled out of the lot. "Fresh air's good for them, so is running and screaming. It gets rid of the wiggles."

The roads weren't too bad, and the county road that led to the school had been salted and sanded. Two more cars passed them, going in the opposite direction. People were out and about again. Brody slowed to a crawl before turning into the school's lot. They found a parking space close to the playground and waited.

"Have you had a chance to show Aiden how to punch?" Harmony asked.

Brody's pale eyes gleamed. "Ian and I spent some time with him before he left for school this morning."

In a few minutes, teachers led kids from the building, and Brody pointed to Aiden in one of the lines. "There's our boy."

Our boy. Her heart did a little hitch. She liked that. She watched the teacher reach the asphalt play area and wave the kids off. Most of them raced away, but a few girls huddled near Miss Fredericks. She hugged herself against the cold, but bent to listen to what one of the girls was telling her.

A high fence circled the area. Harmony watched Aiden and two other boys head to the basketball hoop. Aiden took a shot, missed, and went to retrieve the ball when a bigger boy stalked up to him. When Aiden bent for the ball, the boy gave him a push, and Aiden fell. Harmony's fingers curled into fists. That must be Dirty Dirk. She stepped out of the SUV, and Aiden saw her. He waved. She waved back and raised her shoulders in a question.

Aiden pointed to Dirk. Harmony glared at him.

Dirk's lips rose in a smug, half-smile, and he deliberately took off his gloves and pinched Aiden. Harmony felt her jaw drop. What an obnoxious little brat! She started to march to Miss Fredericks when Brody stepped from the SUV, went to a trash container, and threw some paper wrappers away. She swore he must have stashed them in his coat pocket. His SUV was always clean.

Aiden's friends came to get him, and Aiden pointed at Brody. "He's the one who taught me how to punch."

Dirk narrowed his eyes, sizing up Brody. Then he looked at Aiden and laughed. "Doesn't matter. You're still puny." He reached over and pinched Aiden again. Aiden's fist shot out in a straight line, straight for Dirk's jaw. Brody and Ian had argued about that—where to hit—but Brody didn't want to get Aiden into too much trouble, so they'd decided the jaw was best. When Dirk lunged for Aiden, he stepped aside, swirled, and kicked Dirk behind the right knee. Dirk fell, hit his head, and his face puckered.

Other boys had come to watch. They all stared as Dirk pushed to his feet and yelled, "I'm going to tell!"

"Go ahead, cry baby! Maybe Miss Fredericks will let you hide behind her," one of Aiden's friends yelled.

The other boys laughed at Dirk, but one of them pointed at him. "From now on, if you touch one of us, we'll all jump you."

That must be Jake. He went to join Aiden and his friends. Aiden looked surprised and happy. Harmony saw Miss Fredericks watching them out of the corner of her eye, pretending not to see, while she talked with the girls.

"You'll be sorry. Just wait." Dirk ran to the swings, shoved a kid off one of them, and took his seat. The kid frowned, looked at the tight group standing together, and ran over to see what had happened.

Brody nodded. He took Harmony's arm and led her back to the SUV. "Our work's done."

She climbed inside the vehicle, feeling triumphant. Brody looked pleased with himself as he pulled away. They headed toward town.

"Do you think Dirk will bother Aiden again?" Harmony asked.

Brody shook his head. "I saw the look on Jake's face. If Dirk's smart, he'll pick on kids somewhere else."

It was only eleven when they reached Main Street with its brick buildings, striped awnings, and old-fashioned street lamps. Brody pulled to a curb and turned to Harmony. "Would you mind showing me the antique shop where you found the cradle? I'd like to find a matching changing table, if I can."

They spent half an hour, looking at chests of drawers and side tables, until Brody said, "This one will work. I can build a top for it and install a pad. What do you think?"

Harmony blinked. It was a beautiful table, perfect for a hallway. It had a drawer that was deep enough to hold pins and changing pads, and its bottom shelf held three deep baskets. If anyone could make it into baby furniture, it was Brody. "It's pretty. It's the same color of wood as the cradle."

He laughed. "Then it's a go." He bought it and she helped him load it in the SUV. "Now, let's eat."

It was a short drive to the diner, and Harmony realized she was really hungry. When they opened the door, the aroma of sizzling meat, grilled onions, and tomato sauce greeted them. A handwritten sign, propped near the cash register, said, "Specials: meatloaf and mashed potatoes, Italian sausage sandwiches, beef and vegetable soup."

The entire restaurant went deathly silent as they made their way to a booth. Harmony stepped closer to Brody, feeling uncomfortable, like she was on display. Then an older waitress smiled and called, "Be with you in a minute. You must be Ian's brother and Tessa's friend."

Brody nodded and studied the people staring at them until they looked back down at their plates and began talking again. One at a time, people came over to greet them.

Harmony wasn't used to how personal interactions were in a small town. Everyone obviously knew each other, and they wanted to know the new people who'd stopped in.

Brody fielded questions with aplomb. Harmony was impressed by how easy he made it look, but then he was a businessman. He dealt with customers and dealers all the time. She was so used to sitting at her laptop, probably still in her pajamas, writing in the privacy of her apartment, the public's curiosity made her uncomfortable.

A worry niggled at her. If she were with Brody, would she be expected to go to business dinners at night? Attend functions at the country club? *Where the hell had that thought come from?* Brody had complained about Cecily dragging him to one social event after another, but surely social events were part of his life, too. She pursed her lips, fretting over that thought.

Brody glanced at her and frowned. He seemed about to say something when the waitress brought glasses of water to their table. She looked to be in her forties. She greeted them with a smile. "Hi, I'm Jules. Hope you're hungry. Ralph's been cooking up a storm today."

Brody ordered the meatloaf. She ordered the Italian sausage sandwich. People stopped drifting to their table to let them eat, and Harmony felt herself relax.

"About that look you had earlier," Brody said. "Something popped into your head. What was it?"

"You're expected to do a lot of social things, aren't you? You're good at it. You've had practice, I can tell."

His expression closed. He was searching for the right answer.

"You said that Cecily dragged you to something every night, but that's part of your world, isn't it?"

He spoke slowly, as if treading carefully through a minefield. "I have some social commitments, yes. It's part of being successful. I belong to three country clubs." He stopped when her eyes widened, and she looked shocked. He pressed his lips together in a grim line before starting again. "I belong to the chamber of commerce, and I have to attend business get-togethers. But I only do the minimum of those. Cecily loved them all."

"How many are the minimum?" she asked.

He swallowed. "Maybe once a week."

Too many. She and her friends went out for beer and pizza every Friday. If they were feeling rich, they hit the Italian restaurant close by or a deli. The dress code meant jeans and a shirt with no holes in it. She probably didn't own anything worthy of a country club. Not her style.

Brody studied her face. "You'd like the people I meet. They own businesses and make a lot of money, but they're not pretentious."

Like hell, they weren't. Rich people were so used to money, they bathed in its scent and didn't even realize it . . . *if* they were nice. If they weren't, heaven help her. She couldn't stand snobby pricks. Her eyes narrowed as she studied Brody. Okay, he was easy to get along with here, but what would he be like in his world? It wouldn't be the same.

He ran a hand through his black hair. "Ian's rich. Do you think he's a snob?"

"No, but he lives in Mill Pond. No one would talk to him if he put on airs."

"Did he put on airs when he came here? Did I?"

This was ridiculous. There were perfectly nice rich people. She just didn't fit anywhere in their world, had no interest in it. She smiled. "You're both wonderful. I'm sure your friends are, too."

His shoulders sagged. "I just got a black mark behind my name, didn't I?"

She shrugged. "Don't be silly. We're friends."

"And that's all it's ever going to be, isn't it?"

She blinked at him. "You knew that. No strings attached. When we leave here, you go home, and so do I."

He pushed his plate away, obviously no longer hungry. Neither was she.

Jules came to give them their bill, and she frowned at their half-eaten meals. "You didn't like it?"

Brody smiled. "We just weren't as hungry as we thought we were. The food was delicious."

She didn't look convinced. "Hope you stop by again sometime. Have a great day."

Harmony wasn't great at hiding her feelings. She was upset, but more, she was mad at herself. What had she been playing at with Brody? She forced a smile and followed Brody out of the diner. The drive home was strained. Brody glowered the entire way.

Harmony dug her nails into her palms. This was ridiculous. She felt like she'd just gone through a bad break-up, but she and Brody had never gotten that far. So what was wrong with her?

Brody dropped her at the lodge's doors, as always, and said, "I'm going to get Ian to help me carry the table inside. We'll decide what we want to do with it."

Good, they wouldn't linger in the foyer. She could retreat upstairs to her room. Her voice sounded too eager when she said, "Okay, see you later." And she hurried inside, practically ran up the stairs, and went straight to her laptop. When life turned to shit, she could retreat into her characters' world. And that's exactly what she intended to do. She'd write like a mad woman and finish this manuscript early. And then she'd leave here, whether her apartment building's boiler worked or not.

Chapter 23

Harmony pursed her lips. She'd had an idea for a scene yesterday . . .

Luxar and Serifina were going to meet with a vampire clan Luxar usually considered rivals. Now, both packs were thinking of calling a truce and working together to defeat Torrid and the army of supernaturals he'd called to their city. Tension crackled in the air as they gathered at a conference table, but Luxar, as always, remained calm and charming.

Listening to him negotiate, Serifina realized he used the same techniques to convince and cajole them as he used on her. It made her wonder. How deep were his feelings for her? And why did she care? If they survived this war, they'd go their separate ways. Still, she wouldn't like it if she was only a fling for him. She wanted to mean *something* to him.

But what if he *did* care? He wouldn't leave his mansion/fortress. She'd have to move to *his* place. She'd be giving up more than she'd realized. He'd add her to his world. She'd be leaving hers. Witches wouldn't drop by his mansion, like they did her place, so she'd see her friends less. Either way, if she was with or without him, the outcome was a no-win for her. She'd be losing something whichever choice she made.

When the meeting ended, and he'd accomplished what he wanted to, Luxar took Serifina's hand to lead her to his car. He leaned close to whisper, "I know a place where we can have privacy. We haven't had time alone since my ex's pack came to my mansion."

Serifina shook her head. "I don't want to."

He raised his black eyebrows, surprised. "Have I angered you?"

How could she explain when she didn't understand her convoluted feelings herself? "No, but we fell into lust too fast. I need to re-think things."

"Lust. Is that all I mean to you?" His expression turned hard, but he didn't argue. A chill emanated off him.

Good, let him be angry. Then he'd keep his distance.

Harmony's fingers poised over the keys when Aiden and Bailey burst into her room, alone.

Bailey jutted out her bottom lip. "Brody's working on a surprise for Tessa. He's too busy for story time."

Harmony nodded. Good. She needed to keep more space between them. "Don't worry. I'll tell him what happens in this chapter when we have supper together."

Bailey didn't look happy. "Will he be here tomorrow night?"

"He hasn't said anything to me. Maybe he doesn't like the way I read."

Aiden studied her. "You two had a fight, didn't you?"

"What?" Since when did she have to defend herself to rug rats? "We didn't fight."

Aiden's lips turned down. "Neither did Mom and Dad. When they got mad, they just stopped talking to each other."

Kids noticed too much. She picked up the book. "Do you want to hear a chapter or not?"

Aiden flopped on the bed, legs up and swinging. "I made a new friend at school today."

"Really? Who?"

"Jake. We played together at last recess."

"Nice. Jake seems like a neat kid."

Aiden nodded, and Bailey climbed onto Harmony's lap. When she finished reading a long chapter, they both took off, and she went downstairs to start browning hamburger. She'd decided to make sloppy joes for supper.

Brody stuck his head in the kitchen and said, "Need any help?"

"No, it's easy tonight."

"Mind if I keep working?"

"Go for it." A sinking feeling settled inside her. She'd been hop-ing they could enjoy each other's company until the end of their stay here, but something had happened, something unspoken. Their ca-maraderie might be a thing of the past.

Chapter 24

When Harmony finished the sloppy joes, she went to find Brody and Ian. She was trying to think of a way to beg out of visiting Tessa tonight. Things were too tense between her and Brody. She'd rather make a sandwich and stay at the lodge.

When she stepped into the first suite, where they were working, Ian was leaning toward his brother, his face serious, arguing with him. When Brody tried to disagree, Ian pointed a finger and pushed it into Brody's chest to make his point. She started to turn to leave, so that she didn't interrupt them, when Brody looked up and saw her. A grin lit his face. Ian gave him a thumbs-up.

The look set her off balance. The man had barely talked to her, had gone out of his way to avoid her, and now he was warm and friendly? She glanced at Ian, suspicious, but Ian looked smug and innocent. Damn the McGregor boys. They were too hard to read.

She cleared her throat. "It's six. I wanted to let you know the food's ready to take to Tessa."

Ian elbowed Brody's ribs, and Brody asked, "What's on the menu tonight?"

"Sloppy joes, no spices, and a big salad." She hesitated, then hurried to say, "I was thinking of eating at my laptop tonight. I'd like to get a few more pages done."

Brody came closer. "Can't that wait? We're giving Tessa the changing table tonight. Don't you want to see how it looks with the cradle?"

She narrowed her eyes at him. "Did you finish it already?"

"It wasn't that hard. I had to stain some boards for sides to hold the pad in place. We've already loaded it in Ian's truck." He motioned to the room. "What do you think? Ian and Luke finished the first kitchen today."

They'd painted the long, open room a soft taupe. The wooden floors gleamed. A small efficiency kitchen sat at one end of the room, a seating area at the other. Two bedrooms opened off a hallway. She nodded. "You've made this really nice."

Brody looked like she'd handed him a gold star. "You like it?"

"A lot."

"Come see the countertops. Formica, but it looks like granite. Almost indestructible." He looked at her. "What would your dream kitchen look like?"

She shrugged. "I've never thought about it."

He stared, stunned.

"My rent's so low, I plan on staying there forever, so no renovations for me. The place is nothing to brag about, but it's cheap."

Brody wasn't ready to concede. "If you *could* remodel it, what would it look like?"

Harmony blew out a breath, nonplussed. "I'm not into white walls. They're fine for other peoples' houses, but not mine. I like cozy more than sleek or modern."

"That leaves a lot of leeway." He snapped his fingers. "I know, we'll watch HGTV tonight when we get back. I have some favorite remodeling shows."

"I thought I might . . ."

Ian patted her arm. "Too late, you've got him started now. When Brody talks about home projects, it's like you and Tessie talking about writing."

Oh, boy. He did look revved up. Harmony watched Brody run his hand over a white cupboard with an admiring gleam in his eyes. She sighed. "I'm going to need wine."

Brody snorted. "Just wait. You'll get hooked on the befores and afters."

She wasn't so sure about that. "For you, I'll give them a try."

His expression crumpled. He looked like he was about to say something, but decided against it. Ian slapped him on the shoulder and said, "We're going to be late, and I'm hungry."

Ian left to help Tessa set the table, and Brody went to carry the sloppy joe pan to his SUV, which he'd already pulled to the door.

Harmony pulled on her coat and scarf and grabbed the salad. When they stepped outside, a wind blew across the lake, strong enough to make Harmony lean forward to keep her balance.

"The weather's going to get bad again," Brody said as they settled inside the vehicle. "More wind and snow."

"I'm blaming this on Bailey. I think she secretly channels that princess from the movie *Frozen*."

"It's sure been a crappy January," Brody agreed.

Harmony racked her mind for small talk on the drive to Tessa's. "So, I told you about my apartment. Where do you live?"

"In an apartment, but I'll buy a house again someday. We had to sell the place we'd built when Cecily and I divorced. She got half the money—enough to buy a small villa of her own. I didn't want to bother with another house right then, so I moved into a penthouse I liked."

Harmony rolled her eyes. "Does it have granite countertops?"

He grinned. "That was one of the essentials on my list."

They were almost at a crossroads when Brody stomped on the brakes and skidded. They had the right of way, but a box truck showed no signs of stopping. Either he didn't see the stop sign, or he didn't care.

"What the fuck?" Brody bit his lip. "Sorry, I try not to cuss except on job sites."

Harmony eased her grip on the door handle. "That dumb ass didn't even notice us."

Brody backed up to straighten the SUV from its skid and glanced both ways at the crossing. Then he finished the drive to Ian and Tessa's. Harmony was rattled, but once they got out of the vehicle and started for the house, she could feel her nerves settle a little. The wind bit any exposed skin, so head down, she hurried for the door.

Once inside, Brody told them about their near miss on the road.

Tessa glowered. "That's the new guy who uses Mill Pond as a short cut to highway 69. He's a menace, always in a hurry."

"If I see him again, I'm getting his license plate number." Brody stalked to the stove to unload his food. "He's going to cause an accident. You watch for him, don't you?"

Both Ian and Tessa nodded. Brody relaxed a little.

They were halfway through the meal when Tessa bolted for the bathroom. She came back looking pale.

Brody sighed. "Here comes the next phase."

"Which is?" Ian looked at his wife with sympathy.

"Bland food."

"How bland is bland?" Harmony hadn't added any hot sauce or red peppers to her recipe.

Brody held up fingers to keep track. "No tomatoes, no vinegars, no grease, no fat, no spices, nothing fried. Onions are iffy . . ."

Harmony rubbed a hand across her forehead. What the hell did that leave? But Tessa looked so miserable, she put on a brave face. "I'll think of something. She can do broths, right? She can have some flavor."

"Every woman's different. It'll be trial and error for a while."

Poor Tessa. Harmony knew how much her friend loved food.

They called it an early night, and Ian sent them back to the lodge with a blueberry buckle for breakfast. It was frozen, but they'd leave it out to thaw. The wind had picked up even more, and when Harmony stepped out of the SUV to hurry to the lodge's front doors, it pushed her sideways. She had to push against it to make her way forward.

She hung her coat on a peg by the door and stepped out of her boots. When Brody stomped into the foyer, he looked frozen. He rubbed his hands together for warmth.

"Wine or tea?" he asked her. "And I need popcorn. I could have eaten another sloppy joe, but I couldn't make myself do it in front of Tessa. She looked too miserable."

"I'll help you make tea." Harmony followed him to the kitchen. She was too cold for pajamas right now.

"I set Ian's TV in the library to record some of my favorite shows. I have a couple of *Fixer Uppers*, a new *Rehab Addict*, and a new *Property Brothers* to watch."

Harmony had no idea what those were. She watched her favorite Food Network shows on Saturday mornings, but no home shows. "Okay, just remember that I'm a beginner. You're experienced."

"You don't have to know anything to enjoy the shows." He carried the tray with their filled mugs and the popcorn bowls, and she held the doors for him.

She knew she was in trouble when his eyes lit up as Chip, on *Fixer Upper*, started smashing down walls and kitchen cupboards, and his wife—Jo—wanted to install new hardwood floors through the entire house. When they mentioned granite countertops, Brody was hooked.

"They install white cupboards a lot to open things up and make them bigger," he explained. "Do you like the white? Sometimes, they install different colored cupboards as the base units."

Harmony couldn't picture two different colored cabinets, but she got a kick out of seeing Brody so excited. He explained hardwood floors versus laminate versus porcelain. They discussed kitchen sinks. He favored the deep, farmhouse styles. He preferred industrial, stainless steel refrigerator/freezers. He could. They were freaking expensive. She listened to him, never bored, because *he* was enjoying himself so much, and it was fun watching how passionate he was about every part of construction.

When they finished the last recorded show, she couldn't hide a yawn.

Brody ducked his head, looking sheepish. "Sorry, I kept you up too late."

"I enjoyed it. You take it all so seriously."

"I do, but that would be like you talking on and on about writing to me."

"I'd bore you to tears."

He shook his head. "No, I'd like it, because *you* like it."

She gave a wicked grin. "I'll remember you said that."

He gathered up their dirty dishes to carry to the kitchen. "I'll get these. Go to bed. Get some sleep. I'll see you in the morning."

On her way up the stairs, she started humming. She glanced over her shoulder to find him watching her. "What?" She stopped to see if something was wrong.

He gave a little shake of his head. "I like it when you sing."

She snorted. "Only when the volume's low. See you tomorrow." But his comment made her puff up with pride.

She felt like she was floating as she drifted to her room. What was wrong with her? She wasn't the romantic type. But she hummed as she changed into her pajamas and slid under her blankets. She glanced at her laptop. She was glad she was going to write a battle scene tomorrow—no fuzzy, mushy thoughts allowed.

Chapter 25

Harmony tugged her ratty robe closer and looked out the window, her fingers poised over her laptop. Wind still whipped across the lake, swirling the snow off the ice so that the surface was mostly bare. Gray skies brooded over Mill Pond, but so far, there were no blizzards. She pulled up her manuscript on the screen.

Time to write the big, final battle—the allies marching out to face Torrid and his army. Instead, Luxar pounded on Serifina's door, pushed it open, and stalked into her room.

Harmony moaned. Not again. Her characters were pushing their luck. She'd left them at odds yesterday, and they obviously didn't like it. Luxar wanted to resolve things before he risked life and limb. Not totally unreasonable. Would she let him? Hell, why not? She was fond of the damn vampire.

Luxar stopped at the edge of Serifina's bed. Eyes blazing, he locked gazes with his witch. "I don't know what happened yesterday, but it's time we talk."

Serifina raised to face him. "If we survive Torrid, I'll return to my world, and you'll return to yours. I need distance from you, or going our separate ways will hurt too much."

"Then let's change the outcome. Stay here with me."

Serifina wrapped her arms over her chest, hugging herself tightly, protecting her heart. "You've lived for centuries and never taken a mate, only lovers. How long before you tire of me? By then, my world will change. My friends will give up on me. When we're finished, I won't have anything to return to."

"What makes you think I'll *ever* tire of you?"

She heaved an exasperated sigh. "We're different people, from different worlds. Eventually, our passion will dull, and then what?"

Luxar shook his head and pulled her into his arms. "It's more than passion. I want *you*, not just your body. I love you, everything about you."

Serifina stared at him, surprised. "But . . ."

Someone knocked on the door . . .

Harmony bit her bottom lip. What would Serifina say? Could Luxar resolve her worries? Another knock. She saved what she'd written and went to see who was there.

Brody balanced a tray with coffee mugs and blueberry buckle.

Harmony licked her lips. She loved blueberry anything—craved the stupid berries. But this scene . . . She pushed it away. She could finish it after breakfast.

Brody watched the expressions play across her face. "I came at a bad time, didn't I?"

"No, the scene will be there when we're finished."

"Timing's everything. You can't stop in the middle of mudding. I have a feeling that's where you were."

She shrugged, trying to relax her tense shoulders. "No big deal. I'm hungry, and I love buckles."

The quirk of his lips said that he knew he'd interfered, but he carried the tray to her coffee table and smiled, trying to move past the awkwardness. "Should I dish up?"

"Don't be skimpy. I want a big slice."

Brody grinned. "I had the weather station on while I made coffee this morning. We should be okay today, but one hell of a blizzard's on its way for tomorrow."

"Make it go away. I don't want more bad weather."

He chuckled. "I wish I had those powers, but I don't. Tessa wants you to call her this morning. Grams could use some help setting up for a church supper tonight. There's some kind of a flu that's downed some of the true and faithful that usually show up for grunt work. Tessa wants you to go with her to help out."

Harmony frowned. "Why me? Why not you and Ian?"

Brody looked amused. "I got the feeling that Grams wants to check you out. She's met us, and we passed inspection. You haven't yet."

Harmony forced herself to put down her blueberry buckle. She stared at him. "So this is a test? Should I be offended?"

"Won't do you any good. Wait till you meet Grams. That woman's invincible."

Harmony groaned. "I'm thinking that I won't have a lot in common with Grams."

"She likes good people, whatever brand. Just be yourself. She'll like you."

Harmony stabbed another fork of buckle. "I'm going to be setting up tables and chairs, aren't I?"

"You won't get off that easy. You'll add silverware, fill ketchup bottles and salt and pepper shakers. Whatever Grams wants."

"Shit."

He handed her a second slice of buckle. "There's joy in connecting with others."

"You're full of crap."

He laughed. Patting her knee, he finished his breakfast and loaded things up to take to the kitchen. "Have a great day. I'm going to be installing hardwood floors in the second suite."

She shook her head at him. "You must love your brother."

"I do. That's a given. The little twerp knows how to work me. We're making good progress."

She laughed at him. "So we're both suckers?"

"When it comes to relatives and friends." He lifted the tray and left her.

She picked up her cell and called Tessa. Yes, she could be ready in two hours. Yes, she'd love to help. White lies didn't hurt anybody. No, no problem. She'd already gotten a few pages finished. When they'd made plans, Harmony looked at the clock and cussed. She'd decided to make chicken and rice soup for dinner tonight. Light and bland enough to be safe, but it took a little time. She went down to the kitchen and put two whole chickens in a stockpot, added water, celery, onions, and carrots, then put them on the stove to simmer.

"Will you turn these off before lunch?" she asked Brody.

"You got it." He held a rubber mallet and was ready for business. She'd watched a Property Brother install hardwood flooring on TV last night. Brody had his work cut out for him.

She went back to her room and got ready. By the time Tessa pulled to the door at the lodge, Harmony rushed out to climb in the passenger seat.

The roads were still good. They drove to the big, white church in the center of town. Grams's car was already parked at the back door.

"Good, it's unlocked. We won't freeze waiting for someone to open it." Tessa led Harmony straight to the basement where the kitchen and meeting room were.

Grams looked up when they came in. Medium height with steel-gray hair and steel-blue eyes, she gave off an aura of energy. She looked Harmony up and down, grinned, and waved her over. "Sorry Tessa had to draft you for heavy labor, but I'm short of help."

Harmony liked her right away. "No problem, what do you want us to do?"

"Help with set-up. We'll need two rows of tables, eight tables in each row. We expect over a hundred people." Grams opened a deep closet and rolled out a pallet loaded with long, rectangular tables. Two other pallets held folding chairs.

Harmony and Tessa got straight to work. The tables weren't heavy, but it took a decent amount of time to get sixteen of them opened and situated, then they started on the chairs. As soon as they had the tables up, Grams and a friend started putting silverware and glasses at each place setting.

"By the way, this is Iris Clinger." Grams nodded toward the plump woman, who'd recently arrived. "She's Mill Pond's real estate agent."

The woman looked up to smile at Harmony. With sandy-colored hair, probably faded from red, and warm, brown eyes, Iris looked easy-going and pleasant. The deep grooves etched at the sides of her mouth rippled in laugh lines. "What a lucky girl you are." She gave a soft sigh. "You've met both McGregor brothers. I wasn't sure which one of them Tessa would choose when they first came here."

Grams snorted. "No question there. That Ian was just too damned cute."

"But that Brody"—Iris shook her finger—"the boy's steady as a rock."

Harmony pushed the last chair in place at her table. "You can't go wrong with either of them, if you ask me. Their mom must have done something right."

Grams studied her a moment. "Tessa told me you're single."

Harmony laughed, shooing away matchmaking with a flick of her wrists. "I sure am, and I intend to stay that way."

Grams gave a knowing smile. "That's what Tessa told me, too."

"Tessa wanted the happy-ever-after until Gary cheated on her. It's never been a goal of mine." Harmony dragged two more chairs to a table and put them in place.

Grams cocked her head, studying her. Harmony had a feeling the woman could see inside her skull, maybe root out all of her hidden insecurities. "Hmm, you had early issues, but those can be fixed, too."

Tessa came to stand beside her friend. "Leave the poor girl alone. She came here to help you, not to be interrogated."

Grams gave an unrepentant grin. "I don't suppose you two would like to help cook a hundred or so cubed steaks."

Iris tsk-tsked. "The girls have already done enough."

When Harmony's jaw dropped, Tessa laughed. "The special tonight is Swiss steak with baked potatoes. When you do the steaks in an assembly line, it doesn't take that long before you can simmer them in the sauce."

Assembly line steaks. That was a new one for Harmony. But she pointed a finger at Tessa. "Not you. I'll help, but you get sick every time you're around grease and cooking fumes. Find something else to do for a while."

Grams pressed some money in Tessa's palm. "Go buy my new grandbaby a present from me. I was thinking crib sheets and blankets, maybe a mobile."

Tessa's eyes lit up, and she glanced at Harmony again. "Are you sure? If Grams gives you a hard time, you can call me, and I'll come to rescue you."

"Go," Harmony said. "I'll survive."

When the last chair was in place, Tessa bundled up and left. Harmony smiled as she watched her pull away. "She looks like a kid who got her allowance. The money's burning a hole in her hand."

"It's nice to see her so happy."

Iris frowned. "But she was always happy, wasn't she?"

"Not happy like now. She was only making the best of things." Grams led Harmony to the kitchen. "Ian told Tessa that he's never seen Brody as happy as he is now, said he's never heard him laugh so much."

"Who doesn't enjoy time off?" Harmony looked at the deep, plastic tub filled with flour for dredging. Had Grams dumped the entire five-pound bag in there?

Iris slid a sideways glance at Harmony. "The poor dear went through a terrible divorce, didn't he?"

Harmony nodded. "His ex sounds like a bitch on steroids."

Grams's eyes went wide, then she threw back her head and laughed.

"Being around Ian and Tessa has been good for him," Harmony said. "Their happiness sort of rubs off."

The two older women exchanged glances, but when Grams opened her lips to say more, Iris shook her head. "No fair, Tessa won't be happy with you."

Grams pressed her lips in a tight line. Finally, she said, "Okay, here's how the assembly works."

Harmony seasoned each piece of cube steak, then dredged it in flour and passed it to Grams. Grams browned it in a skillet. While she cooked the meat, Iris started the sauce: diced onions, celery, and green peppers, then diced tomatoes, ketchup, and seasonings. The browned steaks went into the sauce.

By the time they finished, Harmony's fingers looked like she'd played in paste. "Does your church do this very often?" It was a lot of work.

"Four times a year. Something different each time," Iris said. "But we usually have four or five helpers. It goes faster then."

Grams took down a huge box of aluminum foil. "All we have to do is wrap the potatoes, and we're in good shape."

"No salad or dessert? Green beans?" Harmony asked.

"People carry those in. We just provide the main dish." Iris showed her how to wrap the potatoes, and those went pretty fast. They were just finishing when Tessa—her cheeks and nose red—returned, carrying large shopping bags.

Saved by baby blankets and comforters! Harmony hadn't realized how long getting ready for church suppers took. Tessa had chosen a jungle theme with monkeys, tigers, and giraffes decorating each sheet, comforter, or crib pad. Grams oohed over the mobile with stuffed animals dangling from strings.

When they'd gossiped enough, and it was time to leave, Grams patted Harmony on the back. "You're a good girl. You'll do."

"Excuse me?"

Grams laughed and waved them away. Going from the hot, steamy kitchen to the bitter wind made her teeth chatter, but on the drive home, Harmony stretched her legs and let out a long breath. Tessa smiled. "Now you know what it's like working in the bakery."

"I don't know how you do it. I don't know how *Grams* does it. How old is she?"

Tessa shook her head. "She doesn't age, and you're seeing her when she's slowed down a little."

"She makes me tired."

"She makes *everyone* tired." When they reached the lodge, Tessa dropped off Harmony and headed for home.

Brody came to meet her. "Have you had anything to eat?"

She pressed a hand to her stomach. "Nothing was ready. It had to simmer a few hours. I forgot about lunch."

"I saved you a sandwich." He led her to the kitchen and handed her a roast beef and lettuce wrap. "The kids aren't coming up for Harry Potter today. Aiden's grown out of most of his clothes, and Paula's taking them shopping."

"Good, I can finish writing my scene."

"Do you want me to cook tonight so you don't have to stop writing?"

The man was so sweet! But she shook her head. She glanced at the big stockpot, sitting at the back of the stove, to cool. "I'll come down at five to finish the soup."

He nodded. "I'll report for kitchen duty then." He took her empty plate and motioned to the stairs. "Get to it!"

On the way up the steps, Harmony knew what Serifina's answer to Luxar would be. She'd pull him into her bed and enjoy him before the battle. She didn't know if she'd live with him, but she'd make sure to visit him every chance she got.

Hmm, that made Harmony think. She and Brody didn't live that far apart from each other. New York was going to be even more glorious now.

Chapter 26

Tessa was wiped out by the end of supper that night. The busy day had taken its toll. Brody glanced out the kitchen window and scowled. "The storm wasn't supposed to come until after midnight."

They all glanced at the foul weather. Wind howled, and sleet pelted the glass panes.

Tessa worried her bottom lip. "Grams had her big dinner tonight."

"It started at five," Ian reminded her. "People eat, visit, and go home early. She'll be fine."

Harmony was surprised to see it was nearly nine. By the time they'd gotten there at six-thirty, set up, ate, and visited, she hadn't realized it was so late.

Ian ran a hand through his dark hair, listening to the storm rage. "Maybe you guys should stay here. I stopped at the store before I came home. We're stocked up on milk, crackers, and sorbet." He grinned. "Wifey goes through a pint a day, but she'd share."

Tessa tossed him a look. "It soothes my stomach, and we have plenty of leftover soup, even if Brody ate three bowls."

"I was hungry." Brody's gaze returned to the bad weather outside. "Thanks for the offer to put us up, but I'd rather head back. It's not that far. We'll help clear the table, then take off."

"I can do that," Ian said. "If you're going to go, go, before it gets worse."

They didn't dally. The sidewalks were as slippery as an ice rink. They slid to the SUV and Harmony watched sleet bounce off the windshield. The blizzard had started, full blast. Thank the heavens the lodge was just down the road.

Brody turned the SUV's wipers to full speed and drove slower than a snail. Even then, it was hard to see. They were at the crossroads before they realized it and had made it halfway through when head-lights glared in the side window, brakes squealed, and metal crunched. The air bag smashed Harmony in place, and she glanced at Brody. The left side of his head was bloody. His head fell forward on the bag. He was unconscious.

Oh, please, please, please, be all right. The airbags started to de-flate, and Harmony reached to gently lean Brody against his door for support, then fumbled for her cell phone and called Ian. "We've been hit at the crossroads. Brody's unconscious. Call 911."

Her hands shook. Her whole body trembled with jitters. Adrena-lin? She knew nothing about how to handle emergencies.

A man pounded on her window, the driver of the other vehicle. She glanced at him and her adrenalin spiked higher. The damn, care-less truck driver. She fumbled to release her seat belt. She'd throttle him. If Brody wasn't all right, she'd hunt him down and hurt him.

He opened her door. Her side of the vehicle had no damage at all. Brody's was crumpled and caved in, the entire side smashed, but thank God, it was a heavy SUV, or it wouldn't have survived a box truck.

The man started speaking right away. "I didn't see you! I glanced both ways, but the storm was too bad. I'm not sure you had your lights on."

Idiot! "They were on. You were just going too fast to see them." She wasn't sure her legs would hold her, and she leaned against the hood. It took a few moments before she felt stable.

The driver kept talking. "Hey, anyone could have an accident on a night like this. I didn't see you. I couldn't stop in time."

She quit listening and glanced through the windshield at Brody. *Please, ambulance, get here!*

"You can't blame me for this," the man said.

Was he nuts? She just wanted him to shut up. "No one barrels down a road when they can't see ten feet ahead of them. You almost hit us last night. You didn't stop for the sign and drive too fast."

The man stalked away to open Brody's door and pull him out.

"Don't touch him!" Harmony ran to wedge herself between the driver and the SUV. "Keep away from him. He shouldn't be moved."

"Cool your jets, lady. He's leaning against shattered glass. That can't be good." He put out an arm to push her aside. He was her height, but stocky. She tried to root herself in place.

Headlights stopped behind the SUV, and Ian rushed to Harmony. She pointed to the truck driver. "He's trying to move Brody."

"I wouldn't do that." Ian straightened to his full height, and the man took a step back from them.

"I was just trying to make him more comfortable."

"If he has a broken rib or bone, you'll make him worse. The EMS should be here soon." Ian turned to scan Harmony. "Are you okay?"

She nodded, but tears misted her eyes and emotion clogged her throat. "Brody's bleeding."

A deep gash oozed blood along his left temple. The driver pinched his lips together and paced in a small circle. "I don't need this shit. It's not my fault I couldn't see his car. My boss said he'd fire me if I had one more accident, but this isn't fair."

Ian's warm brown eyes flashed with temper. "Just shut up. All you think about is yourself."

"Hey, man—" Luckily, his words were cut off by the sound of a siren.

Harmony stepped out of the way to let the experts do their job. She looked away when they lifted a limp Brody from the SUV and strapped him on a gurney. They were wheeling him away when he opened his eyes, frowned, and said, "Where's Harmony?"

She hurried forward so that he could see her. "I'm here. I'm fine."

"Stay with me."

She blinked, surprised. "Ian's here."

"I want you."

She glanced at the tech, unsure.

He shrugged. "Grams is a good friend of mine. He's not critical. If you want to ride with him, I'm down with it."

She sat next to his gurney on the way to the hospital, and he never let go of her hand.

"My insurance information's on a card in my wallet," he told her. "They'll ask for that."

When they rolled him into the emergency room, she sat in the lobby, waiting for Ian's arrival. So many emotions churned through her, she had trouble sorting them. Fear. Worry. Anger. And deep, deep down, a sort of numbness. Brody could have been killed. She could have lost him.

Ian stalked through the doors a short time later. "Sorry, I had to stay to talk to the deputy and make a statement. Glad I did. The box truck driver kept insisting Brody didn't have his headlights on."

That didn't surprise her. The man was a jerk.

"How's he doing?" Ian asked.

"Too soon to be sure, but the EMT thought he had a broken arm."

Ian winced. "He took a beating. Thanks for staying with him."

"I'm glad they let me." She bit her bottom lip. "The worry would have driven me crazy if they hadn't."

"Tess wanted to come, but I talked her out of it. I don't want her out on these roads tonight. I can give you a ride home when they kick us out of here."

Harmony nodded, only half taking in what he said. She kept seeing Brody, slumped against the side of the SUV, blood oozing from his temple. What would she have done if she'd lost him? The thought stopped her. She couldn't go there.

A doctor walked toward them, giving off an air of authority and calm. "Brody's being taken to his room now. You can visit him in a few minutes. His ribs are severely bruised, and he'll have to take pain medication so he can breathe normally. And his left arm was broken. It's in a cast. His head wound was minor, and there's no concussion, but we're going to keep him overnight for observation. He won't be able to do his usual work for a few weeks, but all in all, he got lucky. Everything will heal."

Harmony felt air gush from her in relief. Ian stood and shook the doctor's hand, then called Tessa to tell her the news. When they gathered their things to go to Brody's room, Harmony kept clenching and unclenching the fingers on her left hand. Brody was all right. She kept repeating it in her head.

By the time they reached the room, the nurse was just leaving. She gave them a bright smile and said, "He's all settled. He shouldn't laugh or cough. It will cause him a lot of pain, but he keeps asking for Harmony."

Ian turned to Harmony with a smile. "My brother thinks the world of you."

She didn't know what to say. "He's pretty great himself."

When they entered the room, Harmony tried to hide a gasp. Brody looked terrible. The left side of his face and neck were covered with bruises.

Ian, as always, stayed upbeat. "The doc says you're going to live. I wasn't too worried. Only the good die young."

Brody shook his head and winced. He reached for Harmony's hand, and she went to sit next to his bed, gripping his hand firmly in her own. "I won't be able to lay the rest of the floors."

Ian sighed. "I watched you. So did Luther. We can manage."

Brody gave his brother a skeptical look. Clearly, he didn't think they'd do the job he did.

Serious for a moment, Ian said, "Look, I'm just glad you're not in worse shape. A damn box truck hit you."

Brody tried to turn to see Harmony and gritted his teeth. "Are you all right?"

"Not even a scratch." She stood up and walked to the end of his bed, so he could see her. There, she turned in a circle and said, "See? The air bag held me in place."

Ian narrowed his eyes. "When I get home, Tessa's old pickup is history. She's getting the heaviest, safest vehicle on the road with a dozen air bags spaced everywhere."

Before they could reply, the nurse returned to the room. She gave Brody another bright smile. "Time for your pain meds." She pushed meds through a hypodermic, then busied herself at a computer mounted on the wall. She kept glancing at Brody as she entered information and smiled when his head sank deep into his pillow and his eyes shut.

"He'll sleep for the rest of the night," she told Ian and Harmony. "You two might as well go home and get some rest, too. His muscle and body aches are going to be horrible tomorrow."

Harmony realized that she was exhausted. By the time she and Ian made it to his pickup, she could hardly move her limbs. Must be the crash after the adrenalin rush. On the ride home, they didn't talk, and Harmony realized that Ian was as emotionally depleted as she was.

"You're welcome to spend the night at our place," he offered, but Harmony shook her head. She needed time by herself. He dropped her off at the lodge and drove home.

Harmony went straight to the kitchen and carried a bottle of wine to her room. After a glass, she crawled into bed and crashed hard.

She woke at eight, got ready, and grabbed her laptop. Ian was nowhere to be seen, so she called Tessa. "I'm driving to the hospital to spend a couple of hours with Brody. I'll probably grab lunch in town, so tell Ian and Paula not to worry about me."

"The roads are better now," Tessa said. "The salt and sand trucks have been out. Tell Brody we'll be up later."

Harmony was tense on the drive to town. The accident made her wary of every intersection she drove through. When she walked into Brody's room, he smiled at her.

"Whenever the doctor signs the form, I get to go home today. I can't work, and I'll be on pain meds, but I can supervise."

"Lucky Ian."

Brody started to laugh, but groaned instead. "Damn that hurts."

"Getting released from a hospital can take a while. I brought my laptop. Want to watch Harry Potter?"

His pale eyes gleamed. "Thanks for coming. I'm cutting into your writing time."

"I've made good progress. I'll hit my deadline, no problems." Brody was more important than a damned book. She scooted her chair close and rested her laptop on his bed tray. They were watching *The Order of the Phoenix* when footsteps hurried down the hall. The door flew open, and a woman with long, wavy red hair burst into the room.

Ian trailed behind her and sent his brother an apologetic look. He smiled at Harmony, but the woman paid her no mind. She stalked straight to Brody's bed. "I came to take you home."

Brody looked startled. "I'm not finished here."

"Yes, you are. Ian told me that he can hire Luther to help wrap up the job. The heavy stuff's done."

Brody crossed his arms over his chest, not easy with a cast and sling. "I'm staying, Bridge. I have a broken arm. I'm not a cripple."

Bridge. Finally, things fell into place for Harmony. The fierce McGregor sister with the fiery temper and red hair.

Brody glanced at Harmony to make introductions, but Bridget ignored him. "Maeve and I are going to take turns staying at your apartment with you. We'll have you in good shape in no time."

Brody's expression turned stubborn. "You're not listening to me. I'm *staying*."

Bridget blinked, surprised. "You never did like being told what to do, but the insurance company told Ian that your SUV is totaled. You don't need to stay to collect it. We can get airline tickets, and you can fly back with me. Mom's worried."

"I'll call Mom. My voice still works."

Bridget narrowed her eyes. "There's something else going on here. Something you're not telling me." She glared at Harmony. "Is it because of her?"

Harmony could feel the blood drain from her face. She hated family drama. Avoided conflict. She pushed to her feet, grabbed her laptop, and said, "I have to go. Good luck with everything."

As she hurried from the room, she saw Ian's brows crease as he turned to his sister. Brody looked just as angry.

Bridget's voice grew faint as Harmony fled down the hall. "What are you two looking at me like that for?"

Brody's door closed, and Harmony walked faster.

Chapter 27

When Harmony walked into the lodge, Paula hurried to check on her. With a sigh of relief, she said, "You look good. How's Brody? The kids are going nuts with worry."

"He's sore and moving slow, but he gets to come home today. He'll probably stay with Ian and Tessa. His sister, Bridget, flew here to help take care of him." If Bridget stayed at the lodge, Harmony was packing up and leaving.

"You've had your hands full lately. Don't worry about reading to the kids anymore. I'll do it. Heck, story time's made them so happy, I'll enjoy sharing it with them."

Harmony thought about how the kids crawled all over Brody while she read, probably not a good idea now. "Brody's going to miss Harry Potter. He loved spending time with Aiden and Bailey."

Paula snorted. "And you didn't? Brody told me Dirk was lucky you didn't impale him on the school fence."

Impaling was too good for Dirk. She *was* going to miss them, damn it. "You've got really neat kids."

Paula came to give her a hug. "Thanks, they think you and Brody are pretty awesome, too. So do I." With a pat, she headed back to her apartment. "Hang in there."

Harmony went up to her room and tried to write, but she couldn't concentrate. On wintry days at home, when she couldn't settle, she spent time in the kitchen. She moseyed down there and started a big pot of clam chowder. They'd bought the cans of clams on their first trip to the store and never used them. She turned on music while she cooked bacon, diced potatoes and chopped celery and onions to sauté. After adding the minced clams, she sprinkled flour over everything to thicken it while she stirred in the milk.

With the soup finished, she opened the refrigerator for inspiration for a side dish. Unfortunately, near empty shelves stared back at her. But there were eggs—lots of eggs—and milk. She started work on a frittata. If both Brody and Bridget stayed with Ian and Tessa, one small frittata wouldn't be enough. She chose a huge cast iron skillet and filled it with mild sausage and broccoli. When they were cooked and tender, she added two dozen eggs. She started it on the stove and finished it in the oven. While it cooked, she made a smaller version for herself with Italian sausage instead of the mild.

By the time she was ready to take the frittatas out of the oven, she heard voices in the foyer. She turned off the music and went to see who was there. Ian and Bridget were helping Brody into his room. Harmony frowned. "I thought Brody would stay at the house for a while."

Ian grinned. "Nah, all of his stuff's here. Besides, Bridget's staying with us. He's trying to avoid her. Can't stand having someone fuss over him."

Brody took a deep breath. "I smell food."

"I made some stuff for Ian to take home to feed you guys."

Ian wrapped her in a hug. "Tess couldn't have a better friend. I smell bacon."

"Only a little. It's too greasy for Tessa right now. It's in the clam chowder. I just finished the frittata. It's hot."

Ian started for the kitchen. "Is it ready to load?"

Harmony went to help him. "The skillet just came out of the oven."

Bridget followed them and looked at the clean pots and pans drying on the rack by the sink. Then she glanced at the smaller containers that Harmony had saved for herself. "You won't get much of those. You'd better dip out more chowder for yourself. Brody's been bitching because he's hungry."

Ian scooped out another bowl and put it on the countertop before he lugged the soup pot to his pickup. That left Harmony alone with Bridget. The woman pursed her lips, studying her. "I volunteered to stay here with my brother, but he's too damn independent. He said you'd help him brush his teeth and get him into bed."

Harmony blushed. "I can help with his toothpaste."

A knowing smile curled Bridget's lips. "Thanks, I appreciate it. I won't worry so much."

Ian came back with a long cardboard box to fit the skillet in, and Bridget turned to leave with him. Harmony licked her lips, suspicious. "You're not staying to visit with Brody for a while?"

Bridget shrugged. "We had plenty of time to talk at the hospital. I've never gotten to spend time with Tessa. I'm looking forward to it." Ian put his hands together like he was praying, and Bridget punched his arm. "I can be nice when I want to."

Ian gave Harmony's shoulder a squeeze. "Don't let my brother whine too much or make you wait on him hand and foot. And thanks for staying with him."

"But . . ." They were already on their way to the door. Harmony watched them go. Bridget looked too smug, just like Ian could at times. She bit her bottom lip, trying to decide what she was missing when Brody called to her.

She hurried to him.

"I'm sorry." He looked frustrated. "I tried to get up and come to the kitchen with you, and I can't make it."

"Give yourself a day or two. You just got out of the hospital. You okay?"

"No, I'm starving. Hospital food is for sick people."

Harmony laughed. "I think that's the point."

"And there's not enough of it." He winced when she put an arm around him and helped him to his feet.

"I could bring the food in here. That would be easier."

"I'd rather eat in the kitchen. I'd like to be away from a bed for a minute or two." He walked beside her, getting steadier the longer they went. She helped him settle on a stool and he carefully exhaled. "I heard the music playing when we walked inside the lodge. I can't dip you today. My dance moves are busted."

Harmony shook her head. "You don't need moves. I just enjoy your company."

Brody's chest swelled, and he dug into his meal.

Chapter 28

When they finished eating, Harmony helped Brody back to his room. They walked slowly because he tired so quickly.

"I'm not going to make it very late tonight," he said. "Can you help me change into my pajamas?"

She eyed his cast and sling. "I'll try."

His lips quirking, he pointed to the ragged edge of his left sleeve. "Ian had to cut it to slip over my cast. And you know how to unzip men's pants."

"Like this?" She undid the button on his jeans and slid down his zipper. She wriggled them past his hips and let them drop to the floor. "Step out of them," she told him.

She clasped his right elbow to help him balance as he kicked them out of the way. Then she turned her attention to his sweater. Carefully, she worked him out of its sleeves and pulled it over his head. The T-shirt he wore under it came next. And then she almost cried, so much of Brody's beautiful body was bruised. But when she glanced at his face, Brody wasn't thinking about bruises or fractures. His gaze dared her to keep going.

She gave him an impudent grin and worked her fingers under the elastic of his underwear. Then she slowly lowered them, happy to see that Brody was enjoying himself. His cock stood at full attention. She gave it a few loving strokes, and Brody's breath hitched, then he coughed and groaned.

She immediately bent to help him pull on his pajama bottoms. "Sorry, boy, but you'd better stay at ease for a while." She stretched the hell out of his left T-shirt sleeve and pulled the loose shirt over his head.

Brody let out a frustrated sigh. "Damn it, I thought I could work the sympathy angle."

She laughed. "Good try, but you're not up for it."

"I was up, but these damn ribs got in the way."

"You're damaged goods right now. Be nice to yourself."

He grinned. "I like it better when you're nice to me."

Shaking her head, she settled him in his bed and propped enough pillows behind him so that he could watch TV comfortably. He patted the bed next to him. "I recorded more HGTV. Are you up for it?"

"Do you want popcorn? Something to drink?"

He shook his head. "I'm okay."

"I'll get you water and your pills in case you get tired and want to fall asleep." When she had everything within reaching distance, she settled on the bed next to him, and he started his shows. After a new *Fixer Upper*, he said, "You always go for cozy with a French country feel."

"And as long as it has a big kitchen and granite counters, you're happy."

"We could be compatible." He did his best to stay awake for the next show, but Harmony finally shook her head.

"Time for your pills and sleep." She got him all settled and started for the door, then turned around and frowned. "If you need something, I won't hear you on the third floor."

He sighed. "Don't worry about me. I'll be fine. I can crawl to the bathroom if I need to."

Damn, that was good. He was working every angle. "I didn't know you had such a flare for the dramatic."

He cocked his head. "Did it work? Are you worried about me?"

"Yeah, you did a pretty decent job."

"I have a king-sized bed." His gaze never left her face.

"Hell, you've come to my bed. It's my turn to come to yours."

His grin was too big, too satisfied. The man was milking this for all it was worth. But how much could she complain about sleeping with Brody? It was a luxury she might as well enjoy.

He drifted off first, and she listened to the steady rhythm of his breaths. He'd scooted her to the left side of his bed, so that he could spoon against her, lying on his right side. His cast rested on her hip. Being draped in Brody felt pretty damned good.

She didn't realize she'd fallen asleep, too, until his alarm went off early in the morning. She couldn't move to hit the stupid button. His arm was draped over her, and his body was pressed against her.

He grumbled and flinched when he rolled to turn off the clock and hissed when he lay back down. She rolled to face him, a little put out. "What are you thinking, that you're going to go help Ian with the suites?"

He studied her intently and ran a finger down her cheek. "You look so pretty in the morning."

She blinked, taken aback. She was far from lovely with her hair askew, her face unwashed, and her teeth unbrushed. She shook her head. "The meds are messing with you."

He chuckled, then pressed a hand to his ribs. "No, *you're* messing with me, and I like it."

She stared. "It's been too long since you've been with someone. Your forty-year-old hormones are kicking in and you need to nest."

"Like a big wren house? Should I start gathering twigs?"

She slid out from under the blankets and began to dress. "You're ready for a wife and kids." And when he found them, it would kill her.

He tried to push himself up on one elbow, gritted his teeth, and collapsed. She crossed to his side of the bed and helped him sit. "You never told me why you set your alarm."

"Because I don't want my brother and sister to come flying into the lodge and hurry in here to check on me. Bridget's not helping me take my morning shower."

She got his point. She brought him his pills and started the shower water. She wrapped his cast in a plastic bag and sealed it, then removed the tape holding his ribs. Poor man. Bruises, bruises everywhere. She bit her lip when he tried to step over the side of the bathtub. Good lord, he was a prime candidate for a fall. Stripping out of the clothes she'd just put on, she climbed in with him and helped him balance. He had trouble washing with just his right hand, so she scrubbed his back and legs.

"I could learn to like this," he said.

She smacked his hard fanny. "I bet you could. Maybe you shouldn't marry, just surround yourself with concubines to do your bidding."

"Nah, too many women, too many headaches."

She helped him out of the shower and dried him off, then rewrapped his ribs and got him dressed. After she pulled on her clothes, too,

Brody grabbed her with his right arm, pulled her to him, and gave her a hot, thorough kiss. "Thanks for everything."

She couldn't talk. Her breath and voice had left her. Her legs were as unsteady as his. Instead, she stood on tiptoe and kissed his cheek. Then she glanced at the clock. Almost nine. She heard Ian's truck pull to the front door to drop Bridget off. Heaven help her. "Gotta go!" And she raced for the stairs.

Chapter 29

Harmony wiped a tear from her cheek. She reached for a Kleenex and stared at her laptop in disbelief. Luxar had almost died, fighting Torrid. He defeated the evil vampire, but Torrid nearly ripped out his throat during the battle. Serifina blasted the last of the enemy army, then fell on her knees beside Luxar's body. She pressed her hands to his chest and poured healing magic into him. When he grew a little more stable, she and her fellow witches took him to his fortress, and Serifina stayed to nurse him.

Vampires heal, but some wounds took longer than others. Still, Serifina was worried. Luxar's were taking longer than they should. Had he come in contact with silver during the fight? Had some entered his body, lingering to poison him, so that he couldn't heal properly? She was about to call in more expert help when she went to his room in the middle of the day to check on him. He should have been sleeping, but when she cracked the door, he wasn't there.

Her heart missed a beat. Had someone crept into his fortress and kidnapped him while he was weak? In stockinged feet, she hurried down the hallway, determined to call her coven together to find him, only to see him dashing about from the kitchen to the dining hall to his cavernous living room. She started down the stairs and he glanced up and saw her. He froze where he was and looked sheepish.

Hands on her hips, she faced him.

"I don't want you to leave. You'd never desert me when I needed you, so I pretended . . ." He stumbled to a halt. "I want you here with me always."

He was shameful. He'd tricked her to make her stay, but she discovered she didn't want to go. She walked into his open arms instead. He lifted her and carried her to his room. Fade out.

Harmony sniffled. She loved happy-ever-after. Luxar and Serifina were perfect for each other. She saved her work and loaded it onto a flash drive, the first draft of her novel finished. She'd rushed the last fifty pages, so she needed to go back and tweak them, but she was happy with herself. At home, she'd pour herself a glass of champagne, and after the champagne, she'd go to a bar and pick up a nice guy to commemorate the end of another story.

She looked out her window and blinked against the bright sunshine, reflecting off the snow. If Brody were in fit form, he'd help her celebrate. She smiled. He was good at that. This time, though, she'd have to settle for champagne and maybe a decadent dessert. She could go to Chase's bar, and he'd stand in for the night, but that didn't appeal to her. If she couldn't have Brody, she'd rather do without.

Her cell sang out "Oh, baby, baby . . ." and she picked it up. "Yes?"

Brody's deep voice said, "Everyone's here for lunch but you."

She looked at the clock. "Sorry. I'm in the middle of a big scene." If Bridget was there, she'd try to avoid her. "I'll grab a peanut butter sandwich later."

He sounded patient. "You're just trying to dodge Bridget. She's promised to be on her best behavior if you come down. We'll wait for you."

"No, really . . ." But she was talking to dead air. He'd hung up. With a sigh, she hurried to wash her face and brush her teeth, then ran down. She wasn't some teenager whose parents could bully her into putting on her best manners for their guests. Her hair had dried funny after showering with Brody, and she didn't have on any makeup. She walked into the dining room, dropped onto the chair opposite him, and gave him a sour look.

He laughed, then clutched his ribs. "I wish you'd quit doing that."

"Serves you right." She glanced at the sandwich on her plate, and her mood changed. "Philly cheese steak. One of my favorites."

Paula reached for hers. "Good, eat up. We don't want to listen to you two bicker."

Bridget listened to them with frank curiosity. "Do you two always talk to Brody like that?"

Ian nodded. "Men are outnumbered around here. We take a beating. Whoever called women the gentle sex didn't live with any."

"Poor you." Bridget leaned toward Harmony, intrigued. "Ian says that you've been cooking for Tessa every night since she's been sick with the baby."

Her mouth full of cheese steak, Harmony nodded.

Brody asked, "What are we making tonight?"

"You?" Bridget stared. "You don't cook."

Brody's tone turned defensive. "I'm not stupid enough to stay in the kitchen with you and Maeve. You'd criticize everything I did."

Bridget pursed her lips, then nodded. "That's fair. How have his meals turned out, Ian?"

"Since Harmony's the cook, and Brody does exactly what she tells him, it's been great."

"And he listens to her?" Bridget ogled her oldest brother.

"I have to, or I don't eat."

Bridget threw back her head and laughed. "So what are you making for us tonight?"

Brody's gaze turned to Harmony. She shrugged. "The thing is, we haven't gone back to the store. That's why I had to make frittatas last night. We're running out of everything."

Brody's face lit with excitement. "Do you have time to go this afternoon? After you finish writing your scene?"

Harmony could feel a blush tinge her cheeks when Bridget turned to listen to her answer. The scene had been a white lie. "The writing can wait, but can you drive?"

"No, but you can. We'll take your Jeep."

"Maybe your sister would like to go with you and help you cook tonight."

Bridget shook her head. "Nope, won't mind missing that at all."

Ian shook his head, too. "Luther and I are installing a kitchen in the second suite."

Paula shrugged. "Don't look at me. I'm on vacation."

Harmony frowned at Brody. If she said she needed writing time, he'd give it to her, but why not pamper him a little more? If it made him happy to traipse around a grocery store, why not? "What are you hungry for?"

"Can you make salmon?" Ian's tone was pleading. "I love it, and I haven't had it for a while."

"No problem. I make it once a month for James." When everyone whirled to stare at her, Harmony put a hand to her throat in surprise.

"He's my next door neighbor. He usually gets Meals on Wheels, but I like to treat him once in a while."

Brody's shoulders relaxed. He gave her an odd look. "Not many people would do that. It's nice."

"I enjoy it. He's an ornery old coot. Fun to listen to."

Bridget finished her sandwich and leaned back in her chair, looking satisfied.

"Good, you're done." Ian started gathering plates to take to the kitchen. "Luther and I can use your help. We're finishing suite two today. You get to be our go-fer."

She didn't look thrilled. "That means I hand you things, right?"

"You got it, the fetch-and-carry girl."

"I'll help Brody get bundled up, then I'll be there."

While Bridget helped Brody, Harmony ran to her room to get her purse. Glancing in a mirror, she reached for a ponytail holder. Her hair looked like she'd stuck her finger in an electric socket, so she scraped it into an elastic band.

Good enough. She ran down the stairs and went to get the Jeep. Pulling it as close to the front door as possible, she hurried to open the passenger door for Brody.

Bridget helped him settle, then stared at her brother as though he'd sprouted orange spots. "You really enjoy shopping for groceries?"

He fidgeted. "I have the time now. I don't when I run the business."

She patted his thigh. "Well, go have fun then. Honk when you get back, and Ian and I will help carry in groceries."

Harmony drove slower than usual on her way to town. Her Jeep was dependable, but it didn't have the smooth ride of Brody's SUV. She didn't want to jostle his ribs any more than she had to. When she tried to hold his elbow when they crossed the parking lot, he pulled away from her.

"I'm getting stronger all the time. I can walk."

"If you fall on your ass on a slick spot, I'm going to step over you."

He grinned. "You would, too, and I'd deserve it." He held out his elbow for her.

They bickered most of their way through the store. Brody wanted to buy enough to stock a hunting cabin until the spring thaw. Harmony wanted enough for two weeks. They compromised on more than Harmony knew they needed, but enough to make Brody happy. If they didn't use everything, someone would.

The owner's son, Mark, insisted on helping them load the groceries into Harmony's Jeep. "Grams told us about your accident. You got off easy with a broken arm and messed-up ribs. That box truck driver is a menace."

When they got back to the lodge, Harmony beeped her horn and helped Brody to the front door. He grumbled about not being able to carry things, so she knew he was starting to feel better.

"We could hang plastic bags on your cast," she said, teasing him.

"I've seen a yoke for oxen at the antique shop in town," Ian said. "We could strap that on his shoulders and load him up."

"Very funny." Brody glowered at both of them. "I'll be in the kitchen. At least, I can put things away."

Bridget came to help them, and pretty soon, all of the groceries were in the house. Harmony parked her Jeep, then went to join the others.

Bridget was happily giving Brody grief. "Are you stocking up for the apocalypse? We could survive for months if we had to."

"We bought this much last time," Brody argued, "and the cupboards are bare. Maybe you underfeed your family, but we like decent meals."

Harmony listened to Ian and Brody banter with their sister, enjoying how comfortable they were with each other. She'd spent her childhood staying out of her brother's way. Her family didn't banter. Their jibes were lethal. There were only a few items to finish when Brody glanced at the clock.

"I have to go get Aiden and Bailey. It's almost story time."

Harmony put out a hand to stop him. "Paula's going to start reading to them. She said we'd be busy enough."

Brody glanced out the door, across the lobby, to the east wing and Paula's apartment. "Were the kids all right with that?"

Bridget stared at her brother as though he were a stranger. "Story time? What the hell is that?"

"Harmony reads Harry Potter to Paula's kids every day at five."

"Did you take your nap towel and stay for story time, too?" Bridget asked.

"You know I like being around kids."

Bridget turned to Harmony. "You must be a kid person, too."

"No, not really." She did her best to avoid her friends' babies and toddlers.

"But you like to cook and spend time with kids?" Bridget looked confused.

Hell, Harmony was confused, too. Who *was* she anymore? She didn't even know herself lately. She was turning into a freak, some-one she didn't know. At home, she cooked a few times a month, not every day. She saw her friends once a week and only paid the guy who delivered take-out the rest of the time. She felt like she was spinning out of control. "I have to go. I have a couple of things I need to get done before I start supper."

She felt Bridget's surprised stare follow her flight from the room. She dashed up the stairs and slammed the door behind her. She stared at herself in the bathroom mirror. Panic clogged her throat, and she fought it down. What was wrong with her? Did country air turn a person into a fifties icon—the common-sense wife in *Father Knows Best*? How did she get so attached to Aiden and Bailey? How did she fall for Brody? Because, all of a sudden, she realized that's what had happened. She loved Brody. How dumb was that?

She walked to the desk and glanced out the window. The sun still shone, bright and cold. She needed fresh air. When something both-ered her in the city, she went for a walk. She left her room and crept down the hallway. Voices drifted from the last suite, out of sight. She grabbed her coat and boots, bundled up, and left the lodge.

Exercise helped. Her whirring thoughts slowly settled to match the rhythm of her footsteps. Things came into perspective. She loved Brody. She knew that now, but regardless of what the songs claimed, love wasn't a cure-all. Love often wasn't enough. Brody had loved Cecily when he married her, but that didn't make the marriage work. Still, how bad could it be to be married to Brody? She liked every-thing about him. But what they had here was an idyll—far different from everyday life. She couldn't base a decision on that.

The cold seeped through her many layers of fabric and she shivered. Time to turn around and head back to the lodge. When she stomped the snow off her boots and looked up, Brody was standing in his doorway, watching her.

"Time to start cooking?" he asked.

She nodded, hanging up the rest of her things.

"I thought you might jump in your Jeep and run away."

"And let you ruin Ian's salmon? I like your brother more than that."

He didn't smile. "Don't be scared, Harmy. Trust yourself."

She turned to avoid his gaze. He understood her too well. Squaring her shoulders, she started to the kitchen. "Are you going to help, or are you going to use your broken arm as an excuse to play hooky?"

He grimaced. "You're a cruel taskmaster. You know that, don't you?"

"I never said I was nice." She took out a baking pan, and he loaded the stainless steel counter with ingredients to make a salad. While she seasoned the fish, she watched him try to slice carrots with his right hand.

"Hold up." She came to take the knife from him. "You're going to lose a finger. You can't hold the vegetables in place with your sling. It's not working."

"Then give me something else to do." He wasn't leaving the kitchen, she could tell.

"You're in charge of rice." She told him how to cook it, and he measured out cups of water.

There was a small noise, and they looked up to find Bridget watching them. Harmony felt the familiar blush heat her cheeks.

Bridget smiled. "I came to offer some help, but you guys have got this. I'll see you at Tessa's." She turned and walked away.

Harmony bit her bottom lip. She grabbed some more carrots to slice and cut her finger instead. Brody brought her a Band-Aid and fussed over her. Rolling her eyes, she snapped, "I'll live."

When it was time to load everything up, Harmony kept a small piece of salmon for herself and piled salad next to it. "I've lost a lot of sleep lately. I'm tired. I'll catch up with Tessa tomorrow night."

Brody scowled, but Ian and Bridget hustled him into the pickup and drove off with him. He gave her one backward glance as he went out the front door. He was upset, and she felt bad about that, but she needed some time alone.

She took her tray into the library and turned on the TV. The evening news was on, and she watched it while she ate. She hadn't kept up with world events since she got here, and she wondered how life on this planet was doing without her. Someone peeked into the room, and Aiden asked, "Can I come in?"

"Sure." She moved her TV tray so that he could sit next to her.

"Do you still like us?" he asked.

Harmony blinked. "Brody and I think you and Bailey are the best kids ever."

"Yeah, but we're kids."

"That's better than being green slime or flesh-eating bacteria."

He grinned. "You didn't read to us tonight. Mom did."

"Brody's ribs are really sore. He can't hold Bailey right now, and he misses that, but I think your mom likes spending story time with you."

He nodded. "It was nice, but we liked coming up to your room."

"We liked seeing you." She wasn't sure what else to say, but Aiden's attention was caught by the TV. He looked at it and hunched his shoulders. Harmony looked, too. Soldiers in uniform were carrying a coffin, draped with a U.S. flag, off a plane.

"That's how Dad came home." Aiden's voice was small.

"Oh, God." Harmony turned off the news. "I'm sorry you had to see that."

"You would have liked my dad," Aiden said. "He took me fishing."

Harmony smiled, hoping it looked reassuring. "He liked spending time with you."

"Yup. Brody told me he knows how to fish. He said the next time he comes to visit Ian, he'll take me fishing."

Harmony's heart twisted in a knot. Brody would make sure he followed through on that promise. "He likes spending time with you, too."

"Do you want to come?"

Harmony would rather shoot herself. "I can't sit still that long. You guys would toss me overboard."

Aiden laughed. "Are you a good swimmer?"

"It depends how far out you are on the lake."

Aiden reached for the remote. "Wanna watch *Spiderwick*?"

"What the hell is that?"

"A kids' movie. You'll like it."

Sure she would, but Aiden wanted to hang out with her, and they sure as hell weren't going to watch the news. She shrugged. "Why not?"

He went to a shelf and loaded a DVD into the player. Monsters and evil filled the screen. Why wasn't she surprised? Kids' movies were always scarier than she expected. After all, Snow White's stepmother paid a guy to carve out her heart. But she and Aiden were both tired. Before long, they were blinking, trying to stay awake.

She woke to Brody tapping her shoulder. She opened her eyes

groggily, and Ian smiled down at her. "Time to put the kids to bed, bro. I'll carry Aiden if you help Harmony up the stairs."

She yawned and reached for her dirty dishes. "I'm okay. I'll clean these up and head to bed."

"I've got these." Bridget walked into view and cleared the TV tray.

Brody tugged her to her feet and put his right arm around her. "Come on, Sleepyhead. I'll tuck you in."

He walked with her to her room, stopping in the hallway. He leaned down to gently kiss her goodnight. Before he could straighten, she deepened the kiss. When she pulled away, she said, "You're such a good person. Aiden needs you. He's ready to go fishing."

Brody's gaze burned hot, but he shook his head. "I'll come back this summer. I promised him." His hand went to his ribs, and she immediately started to apologize.

"I shouldn't have . . ."

"I liked it. I want more, but not now. For now, you need some sleep. I'll see you tomorrow." He gave her a small push into her room and closed the door.

She leaned on it a minute, then jerked it open. Sticking her head out, she called, "Is someone staying with you tonight?"

"Bridget's sleeping on the couch. I'll be fine."

That settled, Harmony walked straight to her bed, shrugged out of her clothes, and climbed under the covers.

Chapter 30

Someone knocked on her door at nine in the morning. Oh, god, why? She tugged on the clothes she'd let drop on the floor and went to see who was there.

Tessa stood in the hallway with a basket of scones. "Your favorites, with dried cherries and pecans." She had an insulated coffee pot in her other hand.

"Come on in." Harmony went to plop on the side of the bed. She felt groggy, she'd gotten so much sleep, but she'd needed it.

Tessa fussed at the little table, pouring them tea. When Harmony frowned, she said, "I can't have caffeine. This is good. You'll like it."

If it was hot and sweet, she'd be satisfied. Harmony reached for a scone. She and Tessa had been friends too long to stand on ceremony. She bit into it and groaned. "This is heaven."

Tessa pulled a chair across from her. She glanced at Harmony's laptop. "How's the book coming?"

"I finished the first draft yesterday. You?"

"I feel like all I do is sleep, but I'm getting there, thanks to you and Brody cooking supper every night. Only fifty more pages. I missed you last night."

Harmony grinned. "Aiden kept me company." She told Tessa about the news and the soldier's coffin coming home.

"Paula's done a great job, helping them through their grief. I hope I'm as good a mom as she is."

"You will be. Great people make great moms."

Tessa finished her tea and set her cup on the table. Uh-oh, here it came. Harmony braced herself. "Great people make great *wives*, too."

Harmony squirmed. She'd wondered what was coming. Now she knew.

Tessa looked like she wanted to shake her. Brody's sister had red hair, but Tessa's wild copper locks warned of temper, too. "You realize Brody loves you."

Harmony nodded. She wouldn't play stupid. She knew.

"How do you feel about him?" Tessa asked.

"I love him back."

Tessa let out a whoosh of frustration. "Then what the hell's the matter with you?"

"I'm scared." Harmony's voice sounded brittle to her own ears. "I'm so *not* like anything else in his world. We don't fit. It doesn't matter here, but it will when he goes back to his country clubs and rich friends."

"Brody knows what he wants. He's not like that."

Harmony let out a ragged breath. "What if I'm not good enough? What if I suck at being a wife?"

Tessa leaned forward and pressed her hand on Harmony's knee. "But you *are* good enough. You always have been. It's just that no one's ever told you." She stood up to leave. "Don't be as stupid as I was. I almost lost Ian because I didn't want to step up to the plate and claim his love. Don't drop the ball, because Brody won't try again. You'll break his heart, and he'll give up. He deserves better. So do you."

Damn. Would Brody really give up? Because of her? Even as Tessa said it, Harmony knew it could be true. She needed another walk. She bundled up, left the lodge, and started down the driveway. When she reached the end, her Jeep pulled up beside her. She panicked when she saw Brody behind the wheel.

"What are you doing? You shouldn't be driving!" His left coat sleeve draped over his broken arm. The cast was too thick to fit.

"I'm not leaving the lot. Get in. I'll drive you back. A storm's coming." He motioned to the dark clouds overhead. Once she was settled, he turned around, just in time. Sharp shards of snow pelted the windshield. He parked, but didn't turn off the engine.

She frowned at him. "Are you okay? Do you want me to leave you off at the front door?"

His face set, he stared out the window. "Let's leave here. Let's buy tickets and fly somewhere secluded and warm."

"What? I like it here. Why would we leave?"

"Because I'm going to lose you. There are too many extras. You look ready to bolt, and I don't want you to."

Tears misted her eyes. She rubbed at them. "I'm not a coward."

"Neither am I, but I'm tired of being *all right*. I want to be happy, and you make me feel that way, like I have it all."

She dug her nails into her palms, fighting for calm. "I drink. I cuss. I'm sloppy . . ."

He reached for her hand. "I don't care about any of that. I've met lots of women who are supposed to be perfect matches for me, and guess what? I don't feel anything. Harmony, I love you. I want to keep you."

Tears *did* fall. "I'm ugly when I cry."

"Not to me. Never to me." His expression grew bleak. "Be mine, Harmony. I need you."

Brody needed her. Her Brody. So big. So strong. "Okay."

"Okay?" His grip tightened.

"If I don't leap in, I'll get cold feet. I'm scared, but I love you."

His sigh sounded like it was ripped from his soul. "I can call a Justice of the Peace. We can make it official before we leave here."

"Okay."

He pulled her to him, and his kiss made her tingle from head to toe. There was so much more to Brody than she realized.

Chapter 31

They kept the wedding simple. All of Brody's family flew in for it and stayed in the lodge. Harmony thought about bolting when Brody's mom and dad, his sister Maeve and her family, and Bridget's husband and children arrived, but Brody kept an arm firmly around her waist and introduced her to everyone. The best part? They all made her feel welcome.

Bridget put it plainly. "You make Broody Pants happy. What more could we want?"

Paula, Aiden, and Bailey came to watch them get married in the huge lobby. Tessa and Ian had decorated it, and flowers overflowed on every table. Harmony wore a simple white dress she'd found in Mill Pond. Tessa was her bridesmaid, and Ian stood as Brody's best man. Brody had worried that Harmony's family hadn't been invited, but that was her choice, and she was fine with it.

Harmony had called her landlord to give notice on her apartment, and he'd been thrilled. He couldn't wait for her to leave so he could raise the rent. She'd move in with Brody until they found a house they wanted.

"Something comfortable with a French country feel," he told his mom.

"With a huge kitchen and granite countertops," Harmony added.

Brody couldn't wear a tux, because the left sleeve wouldn't fit over his cast, so he wore a suit instead and pinned the sleeve in place. He'd hired a caterer from Indianapolis so that Harmony and Tessa wouldn't have to cook, and there were fancy appetizers, wonderful food, and plenty to drink. He'd stocked up on Harmony's favorite wine. And when the wedding was over, he and Harmony climbed into her Jeep and waved their farewells.

"You're sure you want to drive to my place in New York?" he asked again.

She nodded. "What good is an expensive honeymoon when you can't get in the water? We could play in the sand on the beach, but we could only watch the waves."

When they reached the intersection, he said, "Turn right."

She frowned at him. "That's not the way to the interstate."

"No, it's the way to the Indy airport." He pulled two tickets out of an inner pocket. "Tessa said you'd never turn down a long weekend in New Orleans."

She could feel her jaw drop. "I thought you wanted to go to someplace warm and secluded."

"That, too. Later. Honey, you married a rich man. I can afford two vacations in one year. I can fly you anywhere you want to go."

She leaned over to kiss him. She still wasn't used to an abundance of money. "New Orleans is famous for voodoo. I might put a spell on you."

"You already have." His voice turned gruff. "I never want it broken."

Neither did she. Harmony made a right turn and knew she'd never look back. Her whole life had changed. With Brody, it would be bigger and better.

Please turn the page for an exciting sneak peek
of Judi Lynn's next Mill Pond Romance
coming in November 2016!

Paula Hull walked with Aiden and Bailey to the end of the resort's driveway to wait for their school bus. The kids skipped and hopped, and she had to hustle to keep up. That was the thing about being short. Her legs had to do double time when she needed speed. Of course, if she lost twenty pounds it might help, but every chef tasted as they added ingredients. A hazard of the trade.

When the bus turned the corner, she planted a kiss on each kid. "Have a good day."

"Mom!" Aiden winced. He was almost nine. She'd better enjoy smooches while she could, because next year there'd be no public displays of affection. He'd be too old, too cool. Bailey, six, bounced up and down next to her brother, anxious to get on the bus and see her friends.

"I want to show Maddie my blue fingernail polish!" She tugged on Aiden's arm. He grimaced, but tolerated it. Since their dad's death, he'd turned protective of her.

When the kids disappeared inside the bus and it pulled away, Paula started back to the lodge. Fast footsteps. Lots to do! Her assistant chef was starting today.

She paused briefly to look at the inn's limestone exterior, like she always did. *Lovely!* Because of her look—the stud in her cheek, her nose ring, and tattoos—people assumed she liked dark and dreary. Not so. She was a cozy girl, and the inn's three storied center with a wing off each end, its white trim, red double doors, and tin roof gave off a warm, homey feel she liked.

Move it! she told herself. She huffed into the foyer and lounge. Wood floors. Beamed ceilings. Leather furniture grouped around a fireplace. She barely gave it a glance. Time to switch from Mommy to Chef. She took a deep breath as she headed to Ian McGregor's office.

When he hired her last June, he'd expected business to start slow, hoping it would grow steadily. He wasn't prepared for how popular the inn became so fast. He was scrambling to keep up. So was Paula.

"I'm sorry," he told her. "You've gone from chef to jack of all trades." But she'd suspected that might happen. Startups were always messy. No biggie.

With four suites in the west wing, four rooms on the second floor, another four on the third, and five log cabins near the lake, the inn could hold up to eighty people. Thankfully, it was only the end of April and kids were still in school. Every room was taken—had been since mid-March—but by couples. That meant thirty to forty people expected breakfast, lunch, and dinner in the dining room each day. Once June hit, things would get busier.

She hesitated before she opened the office door, collecting her thoughts. When Alex had died in the military, she'd struggled to hang in there as a chef for a prestigious New York restaurant. But restaurants demand lots of hours and she never saw her kids, so she'd come to Mill Pond to work for Ian. Thank God, the man was married and madly in love with his wife, or he'd be damned tempting. Her boss was a long slurp of eye candy who could hardly wait until his and Tessa's baby was born. Paula smiled, remembering. Alex had been excited when she got pregnant, but not like Ian. The man was already mapping out tennis lessons and fishing trips with his first born.

Fishing trips. Paula sighed. It brought back memories of her Alex. He had been a fun father and took Aiden fishing every summer. The kids missed him. She'd moved here because she could keep the kids close.

"I can offer you the inn's east wing as an apartment," Ian had said.

It had seemed the perfect fit, but then the inn had gotten so popular, she put in long hours here, too. She was still trying to find her way as a single mom, to find balance, but it wasn't easy.

"This isn't working," Ian told her a couple weeks ago, and her stomach sank. Was he going to fire her? Hire someone younger, without kids? "You're working too many hours. You need help." And he started looking for an assistant. Betty came in every day from

ten to two—ready to do anything and everything—but she wasn't
enough. Neither was Howard, who took Betty's place from four to
eight. Ian realized that. He was good that way. He'd even asked her
to sit in on the job interviews for an assistant chef, and they'd decided on Tyne Newsome, just off a long trek through Thailand.

"Here I thought you'd focus on cooking creds," Ian teased her. "I
didn't think you'd swoon over Tyne's looks."

The man was nothing short of gorgeous, but looks alone didn't
trip her trigger. She went for the aloof bad asses every time, and unfortunately, one happened to be delivering the inn's groceries every
morning: Jason.

She gave a quick knock on Ian's door and entered the small room
that held a table and his laptop. Bookcases lined the walls. Tyne was
already seated across from their boss.

"Hey, you ready?" Ian asked, standing to greet her.

"Can't wait." With an assistant, she might have time to breathe, to
have a life.

She took the chair next to Tyne's. *Poor Ian.* He was going to have
his hands full. First, he'd hired her—a Goth mama with a New York
attitude. She'd grown up an army brat, always the new kid in school,
a little on the wild side. Her looks told the world that she was who
she was. Take it or leave it.

Ian took it. "Mill Pond is Midwest, but once they meet you and
like you, you're in. They might balk at the stud, but they'll move past
it. Besides, you're so cute, you can pull it off."

Cute. That had been Alex's word for her, too. She'd never win a
beauty contest, or even be called pretty, but *cute* she could pull off.
"What about the inn's guests?"

"After they taste your cooking, they won't care." And so far they
hadn't. Lots of cooks sported tattoos. Add a stud and a tiny nose ring,
and guests barely blinked, but then Mill Pond was a bit on the eclec-
tic side. Lots of artists and creative types. That helped.

Hiring her had been bad enough, but then Ian hired Tyne. The
man was so hot Ian would have to hang a No Touching sign around
his neck. Over six feet tall, he had tousled, dirty blond hair. A chin
strap beard added a scruffy look. And dark brown eyes finished the
package. Oh, and there was the body—all rock-hard abs and sinews.
Teenage girls would cling to his ankles to worship.

Tyne raised an eyebrow at her. "Any second thoughts?"

"About what?"

"About allowing me in your kitchen. We have really different approaches to food."

She shrugged. "That's why I like you. I don't want a carbon copy. I want someone to make this place stand out."

His grin was as devastating as Ian's. Women would come here just to ogle. They'd be lucky if they didn't dehydrate from drooling too much.

Paula glanced at her watch, immune to their hotness. If they got the intros over with soon enough, she'd be in the kitchen in time to meet Jason when he made his deliveries. Her skin prickled. Her pulse pattered. Jason was no looker like these two, but he had swagger. He played it cool, uninterested. For her, a real turn on.

Ian leaned back in his chair. "We already went over all the specifics. Anything either of you want to ask or add?"

Tyne shook his head. So did Paula.

Ian grinned, dimples showing. "Then good luck to the two of you. This is going to be a fun mix."

That was the idea—Tyne's international fusion dishes mingled with her classic, traditional style. Guests should have plenty to choose from. Mill Pond was a foodie retreat. There were so many specialty farmers and suppliers in the area, people expected more when they came here.

Paula pushed from her chair and Tyne followed her to the kitchen. She had everything ready to go for breakfast. Early risers could choose from cereals or homemade granola, fresh fruits, and rolls or donuts, but most guests opted for a leisurely breakfast at nine. She poured lemon-blueberry batter on the griddle for pancakes, checked the sausage patties, links, and candied bacon strips she'd already put in the warming oven, and started filling ramekins, nestled in a steel serving pan, for eggs en cocotte with smoked salmon.

Ian's wife, Tessa, owned a bakery and made a different kind of muffin each day. Today's were banana with a streusel topping. A toaster sat at the ready on the serving bar in the dining room, along with different kinds of breads, bagels, and muffins.

Tyne watched for a second, then pitched in. They worked in companionable silence until it was time for set-up. "A warming table?" he asked.

She nodded.

They carried everything out, put pitchers of juices close to the coffee urn and hot water dispenser, then retreated to the kitchen as guests came and went. She and Tyne flitted in and out to clear tables and refill empty pitchers. Women stopped, gawked. He didn't notice. In between work, he asked, "Same thing every morning?"

Paula shook her head. "This is the Tuesday and Thursday offering. Wednesdays, I make croissant French toast with a peach filling in place of the pancakes. Mondays and Fridays, I switch to a southwestern strata with sausage, and Saturdays are Dutch babies with fruit filling and whipped cream. I need to start those early while the kids sleep in."

"And Sundays?"

"We serve a brunch buffet. We'll both have to work that one. Betty's helped, but she likes Sundays off."

"Betty?" Tyne turned for an answer.

"She helps anywhere and everywhere, like most of us. Works ten to two, six days a week. Her bark's a lot worse than her bite."

Tyne blinked. "I'll try to get on her good side."

"You won't have to try too hard." He was probably around thirty, like Paula, but parenthood had made her feel older, more responsible. Betty was in her sixties with two grown boys. She'd be tempted to take Tyne under her wing. "You've come to a good place to meet food people."

"That's what I've heard, why I put in for the job. Ian said I could experiment, try to find my own style. Someday, I want to open my own restaurant. Mill Pond should give me lots of ideas."

The clock hit ten and the last guest left the dining room. Paula started clearing it.

"No stragglers?" Tyne asked.

"This isn't a restaurant. It's an inn. We serve breakfast at nine, lunch at twelve-thirty, and supper at six. There are choices, but no menu. If a guest wants something else, there's a diner in town."

"Reminds me of the summer camps my parents shipped me to as a kid, only classier." Tyne's voice had a bite to it. That must have been a sore point.

Paula had to laugh. "Sort of the same idea, only Ian offers golf, tennis, horseback riding, and the lake."

She'd barely mentioned his name when Ian bustled into the kitchen to pitch in with clean-up. Once school was out, a high school kid came to work the dishwasher for breakfast and lunch, but during the slower months, Ian offered a hand. When Betty strolled in, she joined them.

"Tyne, Betty," Paula said in way of introductions. "Betty, Tyne."

Betty cocked an eyebrow. Her hair was as salty as her attitude. "He's too cute to cook. You just chose him for his looks."

Paula sighed. So did Tyne. "I've cooked in more than a dozen different countries," he told her.

Betty shrugged. "So? No girl anywhere would turn you away—except maybe her." She motioned to Paula. "All she does is work."

Tyne rolled his eyes, but let it slide. He went back to helping Ian.

Paula had heard it before. Often. Even though Jason tempted her, it had been a while since she entertained the thought of being with a man. She'd pictured herself as a work horse for so long, she couldn't think of herself as sexy anymore. Alex had loved her curves and cockiness. She had a sharp tongue and a temper, but she'd put everything under wraps when he died. Literally. People would be surprised she had a figure under her chef coat and drawstring pants.

Betty gave a wry smile. "It's not going to happen, is it? Okay, do what you always do. Start cooking."

Paula's comfort zone. She showed Betty the menu for lunch. The older woman glanced at it with a quick nod. "I'll get the buffet table and dining room set up, then start the sandwich fillings. You've already roasted the beef?"

"Yup, ready to go." She and Tyne were slicing eggplants and Vidalia onions for today's veggie sandwich when the kitchen's back door opened. Paula stopped working. Her gaze followed Jason as he wheeled a stack of boxes inside, full of produce, meats, and supplies. Her pulse quickened, and the kitchen melted away as a backdrop. She turned to Jason with a smile. "Good morning."

He gave a curt nod, ignored Betty—as usual—barely acknowledged Ian, then narrowed his eyes at Tyne.

Paula hurried to make introductions. "Jason, our new assistant chef, Tyne Newsome. Tyne, our delivery man, Jason Baxter. I don't have time to go to each of our suppliers every day. Neither do Chase or Ralph, in town, so Jason does it for us. We rely on him. He checks each item, fills our food lists, and delivers them."

"Nice set-up." Tyne glanced at the variety of suppliers' names on the boxes. "Chase and Ralph own restaurants, too?"

Ian nodded. "Ralph runs the diner. Chase owns the bar."

"Where you from?" Jason looked Tyne up and down. "You don't look like a cook. No studs or tattoos like Paula here."

Paula blinked, taken aback. He'd never mentioned anything about the stud in her cheek, never stared at her little nose ring or tattoos. She thought Mill Pond had gotten used to her pitch black hair, pulled up in a clip so it spiked at the back of her head, and her fondness for wearing black.

Tyne glanced at her expression, frowned, then gave Jason a dirty look. "Tats from every country, bro." He yanked his T-shirt up to his chest. Blue ink swirled on his sides. He yanked at his shirt's neckline, and more ink stretched across his shoulders. "Happy?" he asked.

Jason glared at his six-pack abs. "Cooking must keep you fit."

Tyne jerked his shirt back in place. "No, work outs do."

Jason reached for his clipboard and shoved it at Paula, making sure their fingers touched. "Here. Check that you've got everything, then give me your signature."

She rolled her eyes. *Men and their pissing contests.* Zipping through the list faster than usual, not inspecting and counting each item, she signed that everything had been delivered.

Jason turned on his heel. He tipped his empty dolly and stalked out the door.

Ian grinned. "We put your Jason in a bad mood."

"He's not *my* Jason."

Ian patted Tyne on the back. "The two of us might as well disappear when Jason steps through that door. I'm surprised Paula doesn't have a tattoo of him hidden somewhere."

"He's an ass." Tyne went to look through the boxes and whistled, impressed.

Betty whisked into the kitchen and nodded agreement. "That's what I keep telling our girl. Jason thinks he's God's gift to women, but I have more respect for our creator than that. She should throw herself at Chase. Now *that* boy's worth the bother."

"I should have told Jason we were getting an assistant chef." Paula hurried to defend him. "He doesn't like surprises."

Ian finished rinsing the pots and pans. "And you know that how?"

Paula gave an exasperated sigh. "If somehow a supplier's out of something I ordered, it irritates him. He doesn't like to bring inferior products or run behind schedule, either."

Tyne glanced out the window as Jason's box truck pulled away. "Lucky man if he expects perfection."

"And you don't?" Paula couldn't keep the snap out of her voice.

"Sure I do, but I'm not an ass about it."

Ian took one look at her face and threw up a hand to call peace. "Down, girl. It's only Tyne's first day. Don't kill him yet."

Paula sent Tyne a withering look. What did he know about Jason? Not a damned thing. But she needed an assistant, so she fought to calm down.

Ian nodded at the kitchen. "All clean. What needs done next?"

He was trying to change the subject, Paula knew. Not a bad idea. "I thought Tyne and I could put our heads together to plan out menus and schedules."

"Sounds good. I'll get out of here and let you get to it." Ian glanced at Tyne. "A word of warning—Paula's little, but she's a firecracker. Don't get on her bad side."

"I'm not little! I'm short!" She sounded sharper than she intended, but five-one was plenty if you put your mind to it. Her height didn't bother her. She'd love to be thinner, though. Not that Jason was trim and fit. He was a little overweight, too. She adored a man with love handles, a little softness like a teddy bear—cuddly.

Tyne shrugged. "Sorry. Didn't mean to aggravate you. My brother swears I can irritate anybody. Words pop out. I say what I say, and people either listen or don't."

Paula could feel her shoulders relax. She liked people who spoke their minds, as long as they didn't push it. "Okay, let's grab a beer and get started." She went to the refrigerator and pulled out two bottles of dark ale and handed one to Tyne, then sat at the wooden work table. It was early, but restaurants keep strange hours and she liked a beer between sets. Tyne straddled a chair across from her. Ian shook his head and made his escape.

ABOUT THE AUTHOR

Judi Lynn received a Master's Degree from Indiana University in elementary education after attending the IPFW campus. She taught for six years before having her two daughters. She loves gardening, cooking and trying new recipes. Readers can visit her website at www.judithpostswritingmusings.com and her blog www.writing musings.com.